**EAT
SLEEP
RAGE
REPEAT**

EAT SLEEP RAGE REPEAT

REBECCA ROBERTS

Gomer

First published in 2020 by Gomer Press,
Llandysul, Ceredigion SA44 4JL

ISBN 978 1 78562 327 1

A CIP record for this title is available from the British Library.

This book is published with the financial support of
The Books Council of Wales.

Printed and bound in Wales at
Gomer Press, Llandysul, Ceredigion
www.gomer.co.uk

ACKNOWLEDGEMENTS

As always, thank you to my supportive and ever-patient family.
Thank you also to my editors, Ashley Owen and Rebecca F. John. Ashley, for allowing Caitlin to get her foot through the door, and Rebecca for her wise insight, advice and enthusiasm. Sue, Sam, Gary and all the other staff at Gomer – diolch yn fawr iawn. It has been wonderful working with all of you.

1

I've struggled with every class at some point. Even Year 7 became fractious when Owen jammed a pencil into his ear. But every week, without fail, my GCSE class makes me want to jack it all in and crawl under my duvet forever.

I've tried every seating combination under the sun to keep Alicia and Nia from talking to one another constantly, and I've yet to find one that works. Put them at opposite ends of the classroom and they just shout to one another. Alicia has completely turned her back on me so that I can see the tattooed fairy peeping up over the top of her thong.

'D'you hear about Demi having an abortion?' she shouts to her mate. 'I was oh-my-god-that-is-so-not-true but yeah, he told her to get rid 'cause he didn't believe it was his kid.'

'But he would say that though, wouldn't he, 'cause he's a total man slag ...'

'Alicia, Nia, face the front and stop talking. Jamie, please collect the homework from last lesson. *Pawb, dyddiad yn eich llyfrau, os gwelwch yn dda.*'

Today's lesson: *Ansoddeiriau.* Useful, but nothing too demanding for last lesson on a Friday.

Jamie has stopped in front of Ryan's desk.

'Where's your homework, Ry?'

'Up your arse!' Jamie looks up at me, scowling. Neither of us are in the mood to be dealing with Ryan's abuse today.

'Ryan, inappropriate language. That's a warning. Where's your homework?' He stretches in his seat and looks around with a cheeky grin at his classmates.

'Not done it.'

'Why not?'

'Can't be arsed. Mum's not arsed if I fail Welsh. Told me I don't even have to sit the exam 'cause I won't need it.'

I deliberately lower the tone of my voice and speak more slowly. I'm not going to let Ryan see that he's an irritant. That's exactly what he wants to be.

'*Siomedig iawn*, Ryan. You know the rules about completing homework …' As I reach for the detention book, Ryan grabs a sheet of scrap paper, scrunches it up and throws it at me. The paper ball bounces off my stomach.

'There's your homework …'

Just when I think things can't possibly get much worse, I look up and see Tom peering through the shatterproof panel in the door. I remind myself each and every day that it's a pupil's behaviour I disapprove of, not the pupil. Tom grew up down the street from me, so I know something of how difficult his upbringing has been. Despite this, I still find myself disliking him intensely.

'Come in please, Tom. Sit down. *Eistedda, os gweli di'n dda.*' He throws his red behaviour report card onto my desk and takes his seat at the front of the classroom. I'm momentarily stunned, because every single lesson so far has begun with Tom arguing furiously that he should be allowed to sit with his girlfriend, Cassie, and not where my seating plan dictates. I place a pen and paper on the desk in front of Tom and try to ignore his glowering. Sometimes it's best not to draw attention to his lateness or negative behaviour, because conflict is exactly what he wants.

'*Iawn, pawb yn edrych ar y bwrdd gwyn, os gwelwch yn dda.* Today we're revising *ansoddeiriau*. Descriptive words. In English it's adj …' Mary's arm waves frantically in the air.

'Adjaculation.' I bite back a smile. Mary is so innocent, so dizzily blonde that I don't think she understands why the others are chuckling.

'Nearly, but not quite. Adjectives. Can anybody give me a Welsh adjective we could use in our work?'

'*Bach.*'

'*Da iawn*, Lewis. Who can give me an example of something *bach*?'

'Your tits.' Tom flashes me a mirthless, wolfish grin. The class laugh again, but this time it's not so friendly. They laugh a little too long and a little too hard. They want to see my discomfiture.

'That's a warning, Tom,' I snap.

He begins to beat a primitive rhythm on the desk, and before I can silence him, he's begun to sing. Almost instinctively the rest of the class join in, chanting to the tune of 'here we go, here we go, here we go.'

'*Titties bach, titties bach, titties bach …*'

Alicia yelps, 'That's not tits in Welsh. It's *titiau*!'

Tom throws up his arms like an orchestra conductor and bellows, '*Titiau bach, titiau bach, titiau bach!*'

These are the dangerous moments. You've lost control. Your next actions determine whether you regain control, or end up locking yourself in the store cupboard and banging your head against a filing cabinet. Humiliation and helplessness kick in along with the adrenalin. My face prickles, hot with embarrassment and anger. I want to scream at them for their insolence. How dare they? How dare they laugh at me?

'QUIET!' They are momentarily stunned into silence. I fold my arms sternly to show I'm not messing, then I realise that I'm drawing attention to my tits and quickly unfold them. '11Y, one more foot out of line and you're all in detention.' I turn and glare at Tom.

'Tom, you are in detention. Half an hour with me, Monday lunchtime.' He is bursting with indignation.

'Oh come on, it was a joke! No way am I doing detention.'

'You most certainly are, unless you want non-compliance marked on your behaviour report.' He makes a grab for the square of red card, but I'm too quick for him.

'Dad'll kill me!' Tom's dad, Thomas Snr, seems to be

9

grooming his three remaining sons to join the family business, despite Tom's eldest brother being found dead on his doorstep one Sunday morning. Word had it that he broke the number one rule: don't get high on your supply. Thomas Snr paid for a handsome funeral for his son, right down to the horse-drawn hearse and football-themed wreaths. However, he is still the biggest drug dealer on the estate, and well known for punching first and asking questions later. I know that Tom will quite likely get battered senseless if he gets into trouble again, so I take another deep breath and try again to depersonalise the situation.

'If you don't want to get into trouble Tom, then make the right choices and obey the school rules.'

'You giving me detention?'

'The school rules apply to everybody, Tom.'

'So you are giving me detention?' He kicks back his chair and jumps to his feet. 'I'm not having this.'

'Tom, sit back down …'

'If I'm gunna get suspended I might as well do something to deserve it. So not on, grassing me up just for saying tits!' He turns to Ryan. 'You coming for a cig?'

Ryan shakes his head. Tom picks up his bag. I keep my voice level and quiet.

'Tom, I suggest you sit back down.' I keep my distance from him, but he shoves the desk away and towers over me, trying to intimidate me with his eyes.

'Move, bitch.' I'm not in his way. He could go around me. There's plenty of room, but he wants a fight. Just as I'm weighing up the least dangerous response, he steps forward and pushes my shoulders. I step backwards to stop myself from stumbling, but feel my body stiffen, muscles tightening, fingers curling into fists. I'm not going anywhere. I'm not moving for him. Back down once and they'll walk over you forever.

'Big man, aren't we Tom, throwing your weight around?' I look straight at him, carefully keeping my face devoid of emotion. He wants to frighten me. I won't be frightened. He wants to see me angry. I won't let him see me angry.

He is the one who breaks away, giving me the middle finger. He tries to slam the door, but it drags on the torn carpet and he looks foolish as he storms off with his middle finger raised.

'You okay, Miss?' Nia asks.

I turn to the class and force a smile. 'I'm fine, thank you.' I pick up Tom's report card, scribble a note and hand it to Jamie, the most reliable messenger, and importantly, the least likely to be influenced by Tom. 'Will you take this to your head of year please, and notify him that Tom has left the lesson without permission?' Jamie takes the card and leaves. 'The rest of you, grab a dictionary and brainstorm as many adjectives as you can, in pairs. Alicia, where are your writing materials?'

Alicia gives me a contemptuous glance over her shoulder. Can't I see she's busy gossiping?

'Don't need them.'

'I don't agree with that. You're here to learn. Find yourself a pen, please.' I place a piece of paper on Alicia's desk.

'Oh, I got one in my bag.'

'Then get it out, please. How do you expect to get any work done without the proper tools?'

'Yeah but I ain't expecting to get nothing done. It's Welsh, innit?'

Here we go again … 'Yes, it's Welsh, but with a little effort you could all achieve a pass grade.'

'But we're not going to need to speak it, are we? Not round here.'

I trot out my pro-Welsh speech. I know what I say to be true, but saying it for the fiftieth time, it no longer rings with sincere passion.

'You'd be surprised. I come from round here too, and

11

being bilingual has been a real benefit for me. A lot of local employers value and need Welsh speakers ... or if you go to college or university ...' My voice wavers at this point. The exam results in this school are the lowest in the county, and have been since I was a pupil. A good number of Year 11 pupils won't even go on to any sort of further education. Most of them think UCAS is a football league, and Alicia is one of that cohort.

'It's still shite and I'm not doing it.' Alicia turns her back on me to talk to Nia. 'So, yeah, I was telling Zainab that she talks crap and if she won't say it to my face then she'd better watch her back ...'

I go down to her level, but she's decided to be insolent and turns her face away from mine.

'Alicia ... Alicia, I'm speaking to you.' She looks at me. Am I stupid or something? Can't I see that she's got something else going on?

'Yeah, but I'm not speaking to you.'

In a matter of seconds the noise in the class has escalated. A dictionary flies across the room and lands at my feet. I pick it up and place it on my desk. It can wait.

'Alicia, third warning. Detention on Monday. Now go to the Isolation Room please. Take a dictionary with you.' I pick one up and hold it out to her. She looks at me as though I'm extending dog shit on a stick.

'Make me.'

In the minute I've been talking to Alicia, I've lost control of the rest of the class. They are shoving one another, shouting, drawing on desks, singing songs from last night's *Family Guy* ... Deep breath, tackle one problem at a time ... but there are so many problems and I can't hear myself think, and now Sam is stabbing at James with a compass and Alicia is smirking and saying to Nia, 'Stupid bitch, does she think I care if she sends me out the lesson?'

'*Dosbarth, byddwch yn dawel!*' The talk grows louder. They really don't care. I'm losing it, they won't listen, what the hell do I do? Forty minutes to go and they're climbing the walls and I can't get them to listen …

'11Y! I'm counting down and I expect that by zero you'll all be quiet, or you'll be spending your dinner hour with me, all of you.' I begin counting down: 'Ten, nine, eight, seven, six, five, four …'

'… three, two, one, happy New Year!' Ryan jumps out of his seat.

'Happy *titiau!*'

Balls of paper are tossed into the air, most of them aimed at me. One of them lands on my cheek, wet with spit. I hate them I hate them I hate them I hate them I hate them … No, you don't hate them. Deep breath, you can deal with this. You've survived worse. Much, much worse than this.

Just then, Jamie runs back into the room. It's rare to see a six-foot-two guy in a genuine panic. Tom is hot on his heels, snarling with rage.

'This is what I think of your comments …' He rips up the report card and it flutters to the floor. I know that nothing I can say or do now will calm him down. He wants my blood. 'Fuck you, miserable bitch! If Dad gets called to school 'cause of you I'll brick your windows and torch your car. You better watch your back …'

I have no idea how the class react to him, because they blur into my peripheral vision. There is only me and him. There is only seething anger, filling me, pushing my shoulders back and my chin up. We square up to one another.

'Go ahead and hit me, Tom, get yourself expelled, or else fuck off out of my classroom.' Miss Bennett is gone. Caitlin B is back in action, and the B stands for Bitch.

'Did you just tell me to fuck off?'

'Yeah, I did.' Stunned silence from the rest of the class.

'Think you can intimidate me, little boy?' We're almost nose to nose, eyeballing one another. I can taste his sour breath. Back down now and he'll pounce. I roll my shoulders with a boxer's swagger, tower over him, look down on him in spite of the fact that I'm only five foot two. 'I'll say it again, shall I? Fuck off. Get out of my class. Go.'

I watch his fingers unfurl and slowly become aware of the kids around me, all simultaneously holding their breath. I've taken down the alpha dog, I've regained control. He steps backwards, turns and leaves the classroom. From the look on Alicia's face you'd have thought I'd just beaten a puppy to death on the desk in front of her.

'You can't speak to him like that! You're a teacher.'

I've had enough of her crap. I've had enough of her sneering, make-up-clogged face with the narrowed black eyes, giving me evils week after week.

'And you can shut up, Alicia, because I really can't stand listening to you whinging and bitching constantly.'

Her jaw drops. 'You talk like this and expect us to respect you?'

'You don't know what respect means. I am so sick of putting up with your constant crap. Every week I get threats and insults and bad behaviour … I'm done with it. Go ahead, fail your exams, you fuckwitted ingrates.'

Mary shrieks, 'You can't call us all fuckwits! I'm not a fuckwit! That's totally not fair!' Okay, she's one of the few who isn't a complete fuckwit. But she's wrong.

'Life isn't fair, Mary. Life gives babies cigarette burns. Life lets rapists get away with it. Life sucks, and it gives you chlamydia.'

Somebody throws a book. Someone else storms off, trying in vain to slam the door, but the carpet is torn and threadbare and the door always snags, frustrating those in the throes of a temper tantrum. For that reason I've never asked for a new carpet. Not that I'd get one. The headmaster would rather use the budget to refurbish his own office.

I watch two or three students leave, thinking: good, stage a mass walkout. Go, all of you. I give up.

But then I hear, 'You think we like being stuck in this shit hole?' Laura. It's rare for her to even open her mouth. 'None of you teachers give a toss about us. All you ever think about is making yourselves look good, getting us to pass our exams without caring what we do at the end of them ... You never think about what else we've got going on.' I know a little about Laura's background. She isn't the only one in the classroom dealing with a lot of 'else'. Bullying, bereavement, divorce, abuse, neglect, eating disorders ... The weekly Vulnerable Child Briefing always reads like the summary of a particularly depressing soap.

Laura is fighting back tears. Suddenly, I can remember what it felt like to be in her position, and that makes me feel horrible for losing my shit with Tom and for using profanities. For some students, the classroom is the only place they can get away from confrontation, from swearing and shouting and bullying.

I feel the adrenalin draining out of me as though a plug has been pulled, sucking the anger down with it. I suddenly feel cold and very, very weak.

'I'm sorry, Laura. I'm sorry for raising my voice and swearing. I'm sorry for losing my temper and for my inappropriate comments. I was wrong to say what I did.' I'm aware that this is the adrenalin crash, but it feels much worse than that ... as though something has broken inside of me. I want to cry.

I'm aware that some of the students have gathered around me. Suddenly, their eyes are sympathetic. They aren't laughing at me and they don't all hate me. Some of them are like me, and they understand.

Hugh throws a pencil. It bounces off my knee and I jerk, as though the carbon is electrified. I come back to reality as though waking from a trance. Geoffrey, the headmaster, is standing in the doorway with Tom at his side like a docile puppy. Game over.

'Miss Bennett, will you come with me, please.' It's an order, not a request.

'I'm so, so sorry.'

'Miss Bennett, at once please.'

'Shall I go and wait in the staff room?'

'My office. Take your seat please, Thomas.' Tom sits down. I leave a stunned silence behind me.

Ryan whispers, 'What now?'

Nia replies, 'She's going to get boll ...'

'Language, girl!' the Head barks. I imagine him, glaring down at them. I can picture his expression exactly, because he looked at me in the same way when I was a pupil here. I've known him long enough to know that he's in the wrong job. I can't imagine him ever hugging his children or drinking beer with his friends.

As I reach the end of the corridor I hear Mary ask, 'Is Miss Bennett going to be okay, sir?'

'Just get your books out and get on with your work. You've done enough damage.' The damage, in fact, was done a long time ago.

2

I go down to the headmaster's office and take a seat. The air is pungent with air freshener and it makes my eyes water. His secretary glances at me as she answers the phone, but from then on ignores me studiously. No orange squash or cup of tea for those sent in disgrace.

I stare at the pinkish carpet tiles and listen to the noises overhead: high heels tapping, bursts of exuberant rubber-soled shoes racing along polished wood floors, doors bursting open and brisk but indistinct female tones calling out. Suddenly, the white noise of the school is like nails down a chalkboard. I am kept waiting until the final bell has rung. I listen to the evacuation of the school all around me, a mass exodus of bodies fighting to escape the building.

Finally, the Head comes back to his office. He sits down with his cup of coffee, plays with a biro and fiddles with his tie clip. I can tell he is trying, and failing, to compose himself.

'You failed to follow the school's programme of sanctions. You verbally abused pupils and used profanities in front of a class.' He throws down the pen. It bounces and rolls off his desk. 'I said it would be a mistake to hire you, but Mrs Court begged me to give you a chance. Clearly, I was misguided to believe that you could ever be anything more than a trash-talking estate girl whose first resort is to think with her fists. Threatening the boy ...' I open my mouth to protest, to try and explain that Tom was the aggressor, but am silenced by a wave of his hand. 'I don't want to hear it, Miss Bennett! You're a disgrace, and if I had the power to do so, I'd sack you right now. Go home and contact your union. Consider yourself under suspension until further notice.'

He gets up, goes to the door and holds it wide open for me. This opening of the door isn't done out of courtesy, or even as a sign that the meeting is at an end. It's done so that I will have to walk past him when I leave the room, so that he can glare down his beaky nose at me.

When I was a student here I was a frequent visitor to this office, usually as part of a gang of miscreants or a fight club. I've seen this routine a hundred times: how he beckons troublemakers into the office with a crooked finger and dismisses them with a scornful or snide comment. And over my troublesome teenage years I made two observations: firstly, that Geoffrey hates children. Secondly, that he always sits behind his desk when dealing with male students, but with females he likes to look down on them from on high. He'll call me names bordering on slanderous – but I can guarantee that Tom will not have been subject to the same treatment.

As I leave his office Geoffrey says quietly, 'If I were you, Miss Bennett, I would use this gardening leave to reflect on whether you've chosen the right career path.' I turn to face him, but am met with wood. He has closed the door in my face.

I know it's unprofessional of him to call me a 'trash-talking estate girl', but I'm too ashamed to be indignant or to protest at my treatment. I have a horrible suspicion that he may be right. I've been sent to the headmaster's office perhaps a hundred times, but this is the first time I can recall feeling ashamed.

Luckily, Geoffrey's office is by the main entrance and I walk straight out to my car and get the keys in the ignition before anyone else can stop me. I'm sure I hear Mrs Court call out, 'Caitlin, *disgwyla eiliad*', but nothing can keep me inside that building. I should never have come back.

At home, I throw myself onto the duvet and bury my face in the polyester. The tears come like a nosebleed. I reach for the bottle of vodka I was given by a misguided Secret Santa and bite down on the rim of the bottle. It tastes like liquid hatred and burns its way down into my stomach. I suck my teeth and judder. Remorse for being like Dad lasts for only a second, and then the opiate soothes the monster.

A quarter of a bottle later and I'm interrupted by a knock on the door. I ignore it. This isn't a pity-party, it's a pity-meal-for-one. However, my visitor refuses to take the hint. The handle turns and the door opens. It's Mrs Court.

'You weren't answering your phone. I was worried about you.' Her eyes linger on the tumbler and vodka bottle. No mixer. Her forehead puckers, but I see from her tired blue eyes that she is anxious rather than angry. 'What happened, Caitlin?'

'You've come to bollock me. I deserve it. But believe me, you can't hate me more than I already hate myself.'

'I don't hate you, and I think you've had enough of a talking to from Geoffrey.' Clearly, she has already heard the details. I'm glad that I don't have to repeat them to her. The memory of his scorn causes stinging blood to rush to my face.

Mrs Court goes to the kettle and fills it with water, then spoons coffee into a single mug.

'How long have you been having trouble with 11Y?'

'Since day one. I've tried praise, detention, seating plans, behavioural contracts. I've filed report after report. Nothing works. Nothing changes. And today, I lost it.'

'Up until today you've remained calm and in control. You've persisted in teaching them a subject they don't want to learn, and because of that they've raised the stakes accordingly ...'

'But what did I sound like? How the hell can they respect a teacher who sounds like a gobby kid? What hurts is that the headmaster is right. I'm not a teacher.' She places the coffee in front of me.

'Of course you're a teacher!' She slides into the seat opposite me, taking my right hand between both of hers. Her hands are soft like a grandmother's. Mrs Court is made of steel, but there is always the faintest scent of lavender about her. She waits patiently until I meet her gaze. 'Do you know why I pushed so hard for your appointment to the Welsh department? There were other candidates with more experience; but I chose you for my department because I remembered Caitlin Bennett, the girl who walked into her GCSE exams with broken ribs. You gritted your teeth and finished the paper. Nothing was going to stop you from passing that exam. That's why I wanted you on my team. Supply teachers walk in through the front door and straight back out again. But with you, I knew I was getting someone with enough guts and fire to outlast the usual batch of idealistic, grammar school-educated, suburban pedagogues who think they can re-enact *Dangerous Minds*.' I can't help but smile, because I think she's confusing stoicism with a high pain threshold.

'But those idealistic suburban peda-whatsits don't kick off and get suspended for verbally abusing pupils.'

'They're usually too busy crying behind the filing cabinets. You were born here, you know the problems we encounter every single day. I know I shouldn't say it, but sometimes it's rather like working on *The Jeremy Kyle Show*.' Mrs Court retired a few years ago, but came back to work after discovering the horrors of daytime television. 'Parents with aspirations do anything to get their children into a different school, and the few potential high-achievers we have go elsewhere, taking their exam passes with them. The school's rankings get lower and lower each year.' Mrs Court takes a coaster and places the mug of coffee directly in front of me, discreetly moving the glass of vodka out of my reach. 'Your strength, Caitlin, is that you are cut from the same cloth as your students. When you were younger I called you my "diamond in the rough". You might not necessarily see your rough edges as a good thing, but I do. You are a role model for every student here. They have siblings, believe me, they will be aware of your reputation. When they look at you now, successful and clever, perhaps they'll think to themselves that they too can succeed. If you could be one of our worst behaved pupils and end up with a degree and a good job, then perhaps the same could be true for them. You can be an inspiration.'

I take a sip of the coffee. It tastes disgusting, but it does its job of sobering me up. She continues, 'I want you to understand that what happened today must be an isolated incident. You've done well to go six months without any real trouble, but if pupils are continually disruptive, send them down the corridor to me. Don't let them threaten you. Don't struggle on alone and risk your personal safety. If they are winding you up, step out of the classroom and seek help. After all, nobody expects you to be perfect after six months' teaching. What we do expect is that you're willing to learn from your mistakes and move on.' She hesitates. 'I also want you to consider seeking help.' She means anger management. 'I want you to talk to someone in occupational health at County Hall. We're not going to force you to do anything, Caitlin, but if you'd let me book you an appointment, I think it would help.'

I shake my head. 'I'm not going back.'

'Oh Caitlin, you don't mean that! After all your hard work, your years of training ... don't throw that away ...'

'The kids have got that place nailed. They're right about the Head. He doesn't care about anything other than making himself look good. Teachers get pushed and pushed and pushed and get no support, until we break down or walk out and don't come back. We have one Additional Needs teacher for 1,000 pupils and our behaviour management system is a joke. Sure, we have a Vulnerable Child List, but we have no idea how to actually *help* those students! We treat them like dumb animals, ignore their problems, throw them into a classroom with thirty other bodies and then wonder why they kick off! Things were crap when I was a pupil, and they've barely improved. All we're doing is forcing kids to conform to a system of sit-down-and-be-quiet!'

Mrs Court waits for me to pause for breath. 'You have every right to be angry, Caitlin. The system failed you repeatedly, and you're right, it is failing children this very second. All we are doing at present is firefighting – managing misbehaviour rather than addressing its root cause. Geoffrey is running the school into the ground with his indifference. He has no vision, no passion, and I suspect, no real regard for the people under his care. When I was head of Welsh it used to make me so angry, having to stand by and watch youngsters like yourself being damaged when they needed to be protected, and robbed of their opportunities by teachers who couldn't teach. I realised that I couldn't walk away and leave things in such a mess.' Mrs Court bends down and retrieves the black leather briefcase that is always at her side. From it comes a folder, the white label left blank. It bulges with papers, sentences highlighted in fluorescent colours, Post-its jutting out from between the pages. 'That is why I became deputy headmistress. As long as my health is good, I've another decade left in me. Leave Geoffrey to me. I'm convinced that soon the school will sink so low that those higher up will realise how poor a leader he is. Once I've applied for his position myself, I need teachers like you to help me – passionate teachers who care deeply about young people. Geoffrey might not see your true worth, but I need you. When the revolution comes, you will be with me.' I shake my head, but she is firm. 'Yes, you made a mistake today, but you are a good teacher, Caitlin. You want the best for your students, and right now what's best for them is consistency and a teacher who will invest time and energy in them. You know what it's like to be powerless, and that's what makes you champion young people. Even our most difficult students, you understand their struggles, you relate to them ...'

'I act like them too. What if I snap again? Geoffrey called me a trash-talking estate girl and …'

'Prove him wrong! Don't you dare run away, Caitlin, don't you dare quit on me. Don't lose that fire! You have moved mountains to reach this point in your life. You have bulldozed through every obstacle in your path. If you can harness your passion and your determination, then once you have a few years' experience under your belt, I truly believe that you will be real management material. Stay in teaching, stay at my side, because very soon I will need a right-hand man.'

'Let me think about it.'

'You'll do it,' she tells me. 'You could have gone for a job in any school, but you came back to St. Luke's. You came back here to change things. At the moment you're angry with how you've been treated, but once you've calmed down you'll realise that leaving would be admitting defeat; and I know you're a fighter.' She leans over and deposits the folder into my lap. 'I've put money on you going the distance. You can't leave now, and you won't leave now.'

'What makes you so sure?'

'Because you're part of my masterplan. When I'm pushing up daisies you'll be in my place.' There isn't a hint of a smile on her face. She's serious, deadly serious about this. 'Together we are going to turn St. Luke's around … and then you are going to run it.'

'Me? Run the school?'

'Yes. Headmistress or bust.' Mrs Court gets up and takes the empty coffee cup over to the sink, allowing me a moment to contemplate her proposal. After this afternoon it seems absolutely ludicrous that I could ever be her deputy, let alone headmistress of the whole school. I feel unworthy and undeserving of her support.

But then, in my mind's eye I see myself on the stage at morning assembly. My hair is cut into a stylish chin-length bob, I'm wearing a black suit and kitten heels. I look the business. I see myself sitting in Mrs Court's office, discussing problems over coffee and brainstorming solutions. I see not who I am right now, but who I might become one day. Six years ago it seemed an impossibility that I would ever complete a four year-long Bachelors in Education degree, and yet here I am: Caitlin Bennett B.Ed. (First class with honours, thank you very much.) With another six years' hard work and experience, and some anger management therapy under my belt, it doesn't seem so preposterous that I might one day be able to set my sights on a management role.

This is why Mrs Court is an amazing teacher. She has the ability to make you feel that you can achieve anything you want. She believes, and because she believes it so ardently, you suddenly find yourself believing it too.

Just then the front door opens and Danielle dances into the room, waving a bottle of Diet Coke.

'Hey, big sister, it's Friday night, let's get this party sta …' She stops when she sees Mrs Court standing at the kitchen counter. Her jaw drops, but her arms remain frozen mid-air. Mrs Court smiles indulgently.

'*Noswaith dda*, Danielle.'

'*Nos da*, Mrs Court.' Dani almost bobs a curtsey.

'I'll take that as a hint to leave,' says Mrs Court, as she places another cup of coffee on the table in front of me. 'Leave the headmaster to me. It might take a few days to smooth things over, but I will. Keep your head down.' She nods at the folder in my lap. 'Give it a read. Let me know what you think.'

'I will. Thank you.'

'Take care of yourself.' She leaves as quietly as she came in. I turn to Dani, who is pink with embarrassment, and still open-mouthed at the shock of finding her deputy headmistress at my kitchen table.

'Hey, my lil' sister from my mum's mister.'

'You can't do street, Cat. You're too old. And way too …'
She holds out her hands, making a square with her fingers
and thumbs. I can't blame her. I used to wear ripped jeans
and Doc Martens. I had purple streaks in my hair. Now I wear
sensible brogues from Marks and Spencer and frosted beige
eye shadow.

I go over to the fridge. I feel light-headed from the vodka,
and slightly sick after drinking black coffee. I need to line my
stomach and get the bitter taste out of my mouth.

'You eaten? Chicken Kiev for tea?'

'Have you got any spaghetti hoops?' Dani asks.

'Nope.' I won't have them in my house. I have a memory
of us both sitting on the kitchen floor, eating them out of the
tin and dipping slices of economy loaf into the watery tomato
sauce. They still taste of desperation and aching fingers. That
tin opener was a bugger.

I get on with making tea and let Dani enjoy having control
of the remote. We talk about her appalling taste in television
programmes ('reality' shows are all she watches), and she
pokes fun at my taste in music. We are careful not to mention
our parents, and I don't talk to Dani about work. I don't want
her to think of me as a teacher. First and foremost, I try to be
her big sister. I have to stop being Miss Bennett sometimes.

Suddenly she turns to me, leaning over the back of the sofa.

'Let's go out.'

'Where?'

'Club Lithium. There's a Friday Night Frenzy.'

'That's for under-eighteens.'

'It's an alcohol-free bar, yeah. But loads of oldies in their
twenties go.'

'I don't think so.'

'Why not?'

'Like you said, I'm too old.' I will be old in comparison
with the under-age nymphs gyrating on the dance floor. Plus,

25

there's a strong likelihood that students from St. Luke's will be there, and the last thing I want is to run into a load of students who will try to rile me.

'Don't be boring.'

'I had a rough day.'

Dani pouts, but I'm not a teenage boy to be won over by puckered cat's arse lips and sad eyes.

'If you're going to be boring, I'll go alone.' She flounces off the sofa and slams the front door behind her. She'll be back. Dani is all bark and no bite. Plus, I know that she hasn't got any money.

As kids we were never taught to control our behaviour. We acted on impulse, just like our parents did. My nickname in school was Cluster Bomb and I was almost permanently excluded for screaming at Baldy Pearson, 'Come over here and I'll crack you like an egg, you stupid twat!'

The very first thing I did after being appointed as a teacher at St. Luke's was to go to his classroom and apologise for my immature behaviour. I was like a recovering alcoholic – a recovering rageaholic – trying to make amends for all the hell I'd stirred up over the years.

Perhaps that's part of what compelled me to apply for the job at my old school in the first place: the idea that I could go back and undo some of the damage I'd done as a student. Baldy was very gracious and said, 'Let bygones be bygones, Miss Bennett'; but he still gives me a wide berth, and I avoid walking through the science department. He's forgiven me to my face, but I'll bet that he's not really forgotten what a little bitch I was. I can't blame him.

Gareth, a boy in my class, used to eat pencils. I can see him now, biting down and crunching goatily through a yellow HB. He'd try and snort pencil shavings up his nose, or squeeze ink cartridges between his teeth until they popped and flooded his mouth with ink.

Then, one day I offered him a pencil crayon and he refused, saying that the doctor had warned him that eating any more pencils would poison him. He'd end up with carbon and splinters in his blood, he said, so he couldn't eat any more pencils or pens, ever. I think that anger is like that. You can deal with a small amount, but if too much of it gets inside you then it stays in your blood like poison, leaving you permanently angry and ready to explode at the drop of a hat.

It's raining outside, and within five minutes Dani comes back, throws herself onto the sofa and glues her eyes to the TV once again. She's sulking because she knows I won't be lending her heels or paying for her taxi tonight. She knows that arguing with me won't change anything, yet she's not ready to admit that she's being unreasonable. We'll sit in silence. Silence hides a multitude of sins.

3

I've been summoned to Occy Health at County Hall. The therapist had a last-minute cancellation, and Mrs Court is eager to draw a line under Friday's outburst and get me back into the classroom. Agreeing to anger management is the fastest way to get back into Geoffrey's good books, so I've signed on the dotted line.

Of course, they don't call it 'anger management'. They usually give it some euphemistic title about assertiveness training or positive life choices. I don't fall for that bullshit any more. All the therapy I've had seems to boil down to the same thing: addressing my inability to control my temper.

I'm sitting in an office masquerading as a living room. The furniture is new and smells of melted plastic. Andrea, the therapist, smiles and nudges a box of tissues towards me. She's one of those women who tents herself in over-sized linen tunics and strings of heavy, painted beads. Without the beads she would blend in nicely with the corporate wallpaper.

She starts by asking for a summary of last Friday's events, and reassures me that most teachers make similar mistakes, especially at the start of their careers. We're human and it's not in our natures to take abuse and allow ourselves to feel threatened. She mentions the reptilian brain and the fight or flight impulse, which I remember from the behavioural and learning theories module of my degree. She explains that some people naturally are driven to escape the scene of conflict, while others are hard-wired to stand their ground.

'There is, of course, a middle ground – assertiveness. That's what we should all strive for.' She pauses, crosses her ankles daintily. 'There's a theory that there is no 'real you', only different versions of ourselves. Our lives are a series of different roles we play out, as mothers, daughters, sisters, friends, and in your case, as a teacher. We talk to our friends very differently to how we'd talk to our grandparents, or someone like the Queen.' I don't tell her that I'm a republican, so the Queen wouldn't get any special treatment from me. She continues, 'We can always choose who we want to be. We can learn to make good choices. That's what I want to help you to do.'

It's easy to be calm and dignified and make good behavioural choices when you're sitting in an office surrounded by pot plants and box folders. Andrea laughs and says she admires my candour.

'That's a very true observation. But I know I couldn't deal with the stress of being in the classroom. I choose to work as a therapist. You have chosen to work as a teacher, and that means being willing to engage with the challenges the job presents.'

She asks me why I took the unusual step of going back to work at St. Luke's? Why did I choose to go back my old high school, especially when I knew the challenges it would bring?

It's a question I'm asking myself more and more often, and none of the answers ring as true as they once did. Truthfully, I don't really know why I chose to go back to work at St. Luke's. It could be down to simple coincidence: I had just graduated and there was a job going in the Welsh department. It might have been because I wanted to show Mrs Court that her mentoring and support had been justified. It could be a subconscious case of 'better the devil you know'. There could be some plausibility in Mrs Court's theory that I wanted to become a role model for young people from similar backgrounds to mine.

The only thing I know for certain is that I decided to become a teacher when I was sixteen. My social worker, Marcus, gave me a pep talk about aiming high, and suddenly I knew what I wanted to do with my life: I wanted to help people, like he did. But becoming a social worker, paramedic, firefighter or a police officer seemed as hopeless an ambition as becoming the leader of a small communist republic, so when I looked around for a way to help people I went in a direction I knew. I had a decade of experience of sitting in classrooms.

'I became a teacher so I could help people. There was a job going at St. Luke's, and I took it.' That's all I give Andrea. I clasp my hands together and stare at her, indicating that I have nothing more to say. Having come up against a brick wall, she tries a new avenue.

'You mentioned problems controlling your temper ... A lot of people find their anger and anxiety began very early in life, usually with their parents and immediate family. What's your family life like?'

This is an avenue I don't like going down. I've trained myself to think about my parents as little as possible, and only in controlled, analytical bursts. My childhood was a white noise of their arguments and aggression, and it took years for me to learn how to filter them out. My parents were to peace and harmony what Brian Blessed is to silence. They are Brian Blessed with a vuvuzela.

I've been to so many therapy sessions, raked over and re-lived my past in horrible, graphic detail. Although I know they are the root of my problems, I've come to the opinion that talking about my parents never helps. I cannot undo what they did to me, I cannot be unbroken. All I can do is try to forget them; try not to dwell on them, not to talk about them, or even think about them unless I absolutely have to.

For that reason I resist Andrea's questioning about my background, and give her only monosyllabic answers. I stubbornly resist all her efforts to get me to open up and confide in her.

Still smiling patiently, she says, 'I'm not sure that you're quite ready to talk about what's bothering you deep down, Caitlin. That's absolutely fine. I'd like to try a different approach, if we may. I think we should practise some relaxation techniques instead.' She reaches for one of the box folders on her desk and removes from it a small paper booklet entitled MINDFULNESS. 'I'd like you to read through the booklet and have a go at the first breathing exercise as homework. Are you okay with that?'

I reach for the booklet, feeling suddenly ashamed. She seems genuinely kind, and I've been uncooperative and taciturn. People stuck on NHS waiting lists would jump at the chance to have access to free therapy sessions, and here I am, wasting time.

As I gather up my bag and jacket I find myself suddenly saying to her, 'I'm sorry if I've been awkward. It's nothing to do with you personally. It's just that I've talked to so many people and none of them have really been able to help. It just seems a bit pointless.' She smiles. She understands.

'Perhaps,' she suggests gently, 'you've not yet spoken to the right person.'

4

I can hear the earth cascading down onto the wood. It's dark in here – so dark that although I can feel my eyes moving frantically from side to side, the darkness is too impenetrable for them to register anything at all. I can't roll onto my side or do anything other than lie flat on my back, and the panic is taking hold. If I twist my torso or attempt to bend my knees I become aware of how small the coffin is. I'm fighting the urge to scream. Save oxygen, I tell myself. Nobody's going to hear you anyway. I begin to claw against the coffin lid, feeling the bare wood splintering under my fingernails.

Suddenly, a phone begins to ring, causing me to shriek. I open my eyes, whimpering incomprehensible, terrified gibberish. I realise that the phone isn't inside the coffin, but on the hall table downstairs. It's daylight, and I'm in my double bed.

I stagger downstairs and snatch the phone from its cradle. I can be quite irate with early-morning callers, but even if this caller is a scammer I am disposed to be civil, because the phone call managed to pull me out of The Nightmare while it was in its early stages. Sometimes I wake up so terrified that I can't breathe properly.

The person phoning is from my union. Or rather, what-would-have-been-my-union-if-I'd-remembered-to-renew-my-bastard-membership. At the start of term I was too busy admiring my new textbooks and organising my stationary cupboard to think about setting up a direct debit. 'Join a union' was always the last thing on my never-ending 'to do' list.

The union official is very nice. He wishes he could offer me legal advice and representation, but unfortunately my membership with them has lapsed, and no, I can't re-join now that I've been suspended from work. He offers me the names of some websites and agencies which might be of use to a suspended teacher, and wishes me luck. That's all he can offer me.

In spite of Mrs Court's promise that she would smooth things over, I'm worried. Six days into my suspension and I've heard nothing from the school. I've phoned a few times, hoping to find out what was happening, but Geoffrey is always 'away from his desk' or 'in a meeting'.

On my third attempt to speak to him, his secretary said rather impatiently, 'You've been suspended for misconduct. I wouldn't start hassling him, if I were you. Stop phoning, stay off school premises and wait till you hear from us.'

He could have resolved this by now, I'm sure. Things moved quickly enough when the trainee science teacher admitted he'd unwittingly snogged a sixth form student during a night out. They were both interviewed, child protection staff were consulted, and he was back in the classroom within two days.

Mrs Court is fairly certain that this is another storm in a teacup which will be forgotten about in a few weeks. The Head knows this too, and I suspect that is why my suspension is being prolonged unnecessarily. He can't push me, but perhaps he's hoping that he'll be able to shame me into jumping.

Over breakfast I read some more of Mrs Court's comprehensive masterplan. If she becomes headmistress I've no doubt that she would revolutionise St. Luke's. I'm in awe of her vision, and the more I read of her ideas, the more I find myself hoping that I will be around to see them put into place.

I practise Andrea's mindfulness exercises, and then after lunch I head to a retail outlet on the outskirts of town. I'm armed with my credit card, but every time I'm tempted to go into the changing rooms I think of a solicitor's bill or a letter of dismissal. I browse for so long that I notice a man is following me, watching me try on numerous pairs of shoes I can't possibly afford. He's either a plain-clothed store detective or else he has a serious foot fetish. I take the hint and head back home.

Later in the afternoon I put on a Puffa jacket and walk to the local marshland nature reserve, where I spend a content half hour leaning over the little footbridge, playing a pretty one-sided game of pooh sticks. I notice an elderly couple of dog walkers giving me odd looks.

'What?' I want to snarl at them. 'Have you never seen a grown woman playing pooh sticks on her own before?' But I don't, because that would be crazy. I glare at them for a moment, just long enough to send them shuffling away towards the memorial garden. I watch them go in their beige anoraks, with their dirty dishcloth dogs trotting at their side.

When I arrive back at home it's only quarter past four, and I'm gnashing my teeth because there's a whole hour to fill before I can have tea, and two hours until Dani comes round to visit. I've spent six days segueing between extreme anxiety and extreme boredom, six days trying to keep myself constantly occupied so that I don't sit and dwell on my own self-destruction.

Six days spent with endless bingo, PPI and payday loans adverts punctuating crap daytime TV; six days eating meals on my own; six nights lying wakeful with the darkness weighing down on me; six days with only the shrill, judgemental voice inside my own head for company. I find myself actually envying the beige couple. They might be standing a few feet closer to the grave than I am, but at least they're approaching it hand in hand.

Later that evening Dani arrives to alleviate my boredom.

'Girls night in!' she says gleefully, dumping her satchel and spilling a small pharmacy's worth of make-up all over the sofa. 'We can give one another makeovers! It'll be fun!'

My suspicions are first aroused when she decides that she doesn't want to do the traditional pampering session, instead opting for a full face of make-up. I oblige, even though I don't see the point of looking like a rock star just to sit at home and share a takeaway. It doesn't take her long to complete my new look because, in her words, the look she's opted for is 'oh natural'. (I think she means *au naturel*.) Touch of blusher, eyebrow pencil, mascara, lip gloss and apparently, I'm good to go. When I point out that she's just recreated what I wear to school every single day, she huffily explains that she's actually slimmed down my face and reduced my eye bags through the magic of contouring, and it's hardly her fault if I can't appreciate the subtlety of her skill.

No subtlety for Dani though, oh no! She insists that I go for 'full-on glamour'. I'm instructed on how to apply primer, contour powder, colour-correction creams and cheek highlighter. (I'm called a dinosaur for asking what's wrong with foundation and a bit of bronzer.) She insists that I go 'full goth' on her eyes, and then wipes the nude lip gloss off in favour of a matte blood-red lipstick of mine.

As she takes selfies to plaster all over her Instagram, I console myself with the thought that far from attracting boys, her OTT warpaint will probably have the opposite effect and scare them away. No one will want to snog a girl who looks like a hooker vampire, right? Then, it occurs to me that perhaps I'm wrong, and the piled-on-with-a-trowel look may be the current fashion. Perhaps hooker vampires are cool.

To complete the look, Dani asks me to put a few loose curls in her blondish hair. She sits cross-legged in front of the mirror and I kneel behind her. It's the first time she's asked me to style her since we were girls, and her soft, limp hair between my fingers feels simultaneously alien and familiar.

35

Her hair is so different to my own. I remember being able to squeeze into the bathtub with her, and standing back to back afterwards, shivering and enjoying the scalp-scalding heat of the hairdryer. Mum always slathered conditioner on my hair and it came out looking backcombed, whereas Dani's hair hung flat and limp after the gentlest shampooing.

Both of us have Mum's bone structure and dark eyes, but Dani is strawberry blonde – so fair that she reminds me of watery orange squash. I once asked Mum where my dark hair and eyebrows (and annoying upper lip) came from, and she said I must have inherited them from my late grandfather. I've never seen a photo of him, but I've always been glad that I took after her side of the family rather than Dad's. I think of it as the lesser of two evils.

Dani was still a child when I left home. I don't know how Mum explained both me and Dad vanishing at the same time, but presumably I was painted out of the picture in such a way that she knew never to ask questions about where I'd gone.

I don't think we'd have come into contact again if I hadn't got the job at St. Luke's. I'll never forget the shock of seeing her standing outside her registration class on the first day of term, chewing, texting, laughing and swearing. Shocked, I also swore, although I managed to do it under my breath. My little sister was no longer little – in fact, at fourteen, she's actually taller than I am.

That first morning we just looked at one another and I moved on to my registration class. I don't think either of us knew what to say. It had been half a decade since we'd last seen one another. But a few days later I saw her walking home in the rain, and I offered her a lift home. Neither of us was sure how to talk about what happened, so in the end, we didn't. We came to an unspoken understanding that my 'disagreement' with Dad and Mum didn't apply to us. We were comfortable in each other's company and gradually, without any big revelations or any deep, emotional discussions about the past, we became part of each other's life once again.

As I reach out and smooth the curls away from Dani's face I experience one of those weird moments where your imagination seems to take your eyes hostage. Gathering up Dani's hair in my hands, I swear that I see her plump seven-year-old face looking back at me through the mirror. Her face is fuller, her bottom lip sulky and I'm scraping her mane into a velvet scrunchie and giving it a good tug to make sure it's in tight. We're playing Whispers, because Daddy is asleep on the sofa downstairs, and Mummy is unwell. It's cold in our bedroom, so cold that I jam a hair clip into my nail bed and don't notice the blood until it starts throbbing later, in the warmth of the science lab. I used to do Dani's hair every morning. It was always my job to get her dressed and ready for school, pinning her hair back with Disney hairclips and buying her breakfast from the corner shop. I tried to shield her from the worst of our parents, but most of the memories we share aren't happy ones. Even our games were defence mechanisms in disguise, always played with one ear and one eye alert for Mum and Dad.

Things seem to have improved at home since then, because despite what happened to me, Dani's name has never appeared on the vulnerable children or at risk register. Her upbringing seems to have been comparatively normal. No unwashed uniform, no bruises or unexplained marks, and she doesn't raid my fridge because she's ravenous. They seem to be better parents to her than they ever were to me – but then, she was always Dad's favourite.

'Ow, you're hurting, Cat.' Dani leans forwards, away from the heat of the curling tongs.

'Sorry,' I gasp and release her hair from the barrel. It lies coiled like a spring against her shoulder. She shakes out her curls and begins preening in front of the mirror. I leave her pouting and taking more selfies.

'I'm going to take my make-up off, get my PJs on and order the takeaway,' I call, going into the bathroom. 'Whad'ya fancy?'

'I'm okay, I've already eaten,' she replies. When I emerge from the bathroom I am surprised to see her standing there wearing a short, form-fitting black dress and stepping into a pair of black heels – both of which belong to me.

'Going somewhere?' I enquire sarcastically.

'Out,' she replies, as though stating the bleeding obvious.

'And may I enquire as to where you are going?'

'Out-out.' She reaches for a little black handbag of mine. How did she manage to go rifling through my wardrobe without me hearing anything?

'You could have told me that you were going out. And you might have asked before borrowing my things.'

'You didn't cancel any plans to see me, did you? It's not like you were going anywhere. I'll be back later.' Tucking the clutch bag under her arm, she almost barges past me.

'Where are you going?' I ask again, as she rushes down the stairs, ankles wobbling as she teeters on the heels. 'Dani, answer me!'

She doesn't, of course. She's out the front door before I reach the bottom of the stairs, pausing only to look back and shout, 'If Mum rings, I'm staying with you tonight!'

'Get back here!' I yell in my best don't-mess-with-Miss-Bennett voice, but I'm shouting at a closed door. I know that as an adult I'm not supposed to be annoyed by her immature behaviour, but I can't help feeling hurt by how obviously she took me for granted. My services as a make-up artist and my wardrobe are meant to be at her disposal, and I'm supposed to offer her a bed for the night and cover for her – but I'm not worth spending any time with.

Enough of the self-pity. The real issue here is that she's gone out dressed like a hooker vampire, she's fourteen going on eighteen, it's Friday night and I have no idea where she is going, or who she is going with.

I ring her mobile, but naturally, she's switched it off so that it goes straight to voicemail. I race upstairs to pull on some jeggings, my Doc Martens and a shirt, and then I leave the house, grabbing my keys, phone and purse as I go.

I set off in search of her, leaving the car parked in the driveway. She may have a five minute head-start, but she is also wearing three-inch heels. It doesn't take me long to catch up with her, so I hang back in the shadows and follow her at a distance. Much as I want to swoop in and drag her back home, I also need to know who she is meeting. She's gone to a lot of trouble to plan this evening – to get herself made up to look several years older than she really is, and to get her hands on a dress far shorter and more revealing than anything Mum or Dad would let her wear. It's a lot of effort for a straightforward night out with the girls, so I strongly suspect that there's a potential sexual liaison involved. If so, I want to know whether he's just another grubby teenager itching to fumble in her underwear, or whether there's something more sinister afoot.

She's walking towards the town centre, and I'm glad that she was sensible enough to choose a well-lit route, even if that brings its own risks. Occasionally a driver will honk their horn, and once a boy-racer type in a souped-up Vauxhall Corsa winds down his window and yells, 'Show us your tits!' I'm proud of Dani's reaction – she just keeps walking, head up, without so much as turning to look at him. At her age, my reaction would have been to yell, 'C'mere then! Show us your dick and I'll rip it off and stick it down your throat!' At one point the driver signals and it looks as though he might be about to park up and accost Dani, but he's only going into the chippy. Bloodshed averted. His penis will remain intact.

Eventually, we reach the town centre. I stay in the shadows as Dani sits on a bollard and massages the balls of her aching feet. She's looking around expectantly, nervously. I edge closer, taking position behind a derelict phone box, ready to pounce if her 'date' reveals himself to be a married father-of-three who poses on Facebook as a sixteen-year-old called Kyle.

To my great surprise, her 'date' isn't a date at all, but her two friends from school, Melissa and Olwen. They squeal and hug one another, and as I earwig on their conversation, it becomes apparent that their intention is to sneak into Club Lithium to watch a punk rock tribute band. I decide to follow her into the club, just to check that their girlish gushing isn't part of a highly elaborate cover-up, and that they aren't actually going on some kind of triple-date.

I watch them going into Club Lithium and from the neon yellow posters plastered around the entrance I see that it's an under-18s evening. If this is all as innocent as it looks, Dani has really gone into overkill. I used to come to Club Lithium's 'Friday Frenzy' under-18 gigs myself; I would have happily dropped her off and picked her up at the end of the evening. Better that, than having her walk on her own in the dark, as I used to do.

The bouncers smile recognition as I approach them.

'Not seen you here for ages,' one of them says, as he takes my five pounds.

'Well, I'm not really your target audience any more. Plus, y'know, I'm a teacher now, so I've had to cut back a bit on the drunken escapades.'

'Oh aye. You should come out on a Saturday night, when the grown-ups come out to play. I might have to give you a pat-down, make sure you're not carrying anything you shouldn't be.' He gives me a wink. I smile my thinnest possible smile and hold out my hand for the admission stamp. Touch me and I'll break your fingers, creep.

I head down the yellow-edged stairs into the club's basement. The air is scented by dry ice, and the guitars vibrate satisfyingly through my diaphragm as the first band finishes tuning up. I stand and let my eyes adjust to the darkness. I notice Dani and her friends sliding into one of the perpetually sticky mock-leather booths on the edge of the mosh pit. It's early, and the floor is occupied only by few skinny hoodies bouncing off one another.

Overhead lights sweep the floor in 'wax on, wax off' circles. Teenagers headbang to the opening chords of the band's set, or neck with one another in the darkness of the booths.

There's something both comforting and sad about the venue, which has hardly changed since I started coming here. Surrounded by sex and drugs and rock ('n' roll), I suddenly feel seventeen again. Before I confront Dani I go into the toilets, and am met by the ghost of Friday Frenzies past. The pink walls have been painted over many times, but you can still make out graffiti carved into the wood of the cubicles. It's still there … Cat n Jodie. We carved it with Jodie's eyebrow tweezers. RHYS IS WELL FIT. That's one of mine too.

It was here, when I was seventeen, that I first had sex with Rhys, the thrash-metal bassist of The Slags, in the dressing room underneath the stage. Wasn't the most romantic first date, but we stayed together long enough for his bandmates to begin calling me his 'missus'. Dates mainly consisted of me waiting back stage while The Slags performed their set, and then we'd go on to a pub or club and spend the night on the floor at a friend's house. He was painfully shy when he was sober, so dates on a week night were rarer and more awkward affairs. We were together for six months before I moved away to start my teaching degree. Our parting was amicable, so amicable in fact that I look back and wonder why we even called it a relationship. I think we ended up together because we were seventeen and all our friends were dating, and also

41

because we were both quite keen on sex. I went blithely off to university, thinking I'd find a suitable replacement in no time at all, but that never happened. Doing a teaching degree meant that I spent three years travelling between university and school placements. I suppose I got on well enough with my fellow trainees, but never stayed in one place long enough for our working relationships to become friendship, let alone anything romantic. People say, 'we'll keep in touch', but they never do.

Thanks to my nomadic trainee teacher lifestyle and my trust issues, Rhys has been my only boyfriend. Nostalgia has lent him a certain roguish, mysterious charm I'm sure he never actually possessed, and I think of him fondly every time I hear the opening chords of a bass-heavy metal track.

I wash my hands under the thin, lukewarm trickle of the tap before going back into the club. The dance floor has suddenly emptied, apart from a gaggle of fans standing at the base of the stage, listening intently to a bad rendition of The Buzzcocks' 'Ever Fallen in Love'.

I pounce on Dani and her friends, and they squeal with shock.

'Cat!' shrieks Dani. 'What are you doing here?'

'Just checking out the band ...' I jab my thumb towards the stage. 'You didn't have to run out on me, y'know. It's an under-18s gig, you're not under-age. I would have given you a lift down here if you'd asked.' I look at her friends, and even though it's too dark for me to see their blushes, I can tell that they're cringing at my presence. I feign nonchalance, glancing around the cavernous interior of the club. It doesn't seem to have changed much since my student days. 'I used to come here myself. Love this music. But obviously you're not going to invite your hideously uncool big sister along as a chaperone ...'

'It's not that you're uncool ...' Olwen ventures, looking terrified. 'It's just that you're a teacher, and loads of kids from school come here.' I glance over my right shoulder and see that she's right. Hell, probably three-quarters of the audience are St. Luke's kids. I decide quickly that I'd better exit stage left, hopefully not pursued by a gaggle of teenagers.

That's the price you pay for living and working in your square mile. Whatever you do, you can never quite shake off the mantle of Teacher. Saturday mornings in town, popping to the corner shop, going to the gym ... no matter where you go, suddenly there will be a gang of kids watching your every move. They don't know how to deal with teachers outside the context of the classroom. Usually I ignore them and hope that they'll ignore me, rather than acting as though I'm some Z-list celeb off a 'reality' TV show.

Suddenly, I'm blindsided by some kid in a hoodie who knocks me off balance. My left arm catches Melissa's pint of coke and it shatters on the ground. I almost follow it to the floor, but flail my arms frantically and regain my balance.

'Dickhead!' I shout, more out of shock than anger. I straighten up and turn around to see Tom grimacing at me from underneath his hood. It's not even nine o'clock but he's drunk, so drunk that his eyes are glazed and he can barely hold his head up.

'I have nothing to say to you, Tom, so please, step away from me,' I say calmly. He looks towards Cassie, then bends down to retrieve the shattered portions of the glass. Blood brightens his fingers. Cassie grabs at his arm but he shrugs her off.

'Just put the glass down Tom and let's go. Don't talk to her.' Tom grins drunkenly, as though remembering a private joke. He places a shard of glass on the table, but keeps hold of the base.

'It's Miss Bennett ...' he slurs.

Cassie steps back, arms folded. 'Tom, you're being an arse. Stop it or I'm going home.' Tom looks up at me suddenly, then back down at the glass in his hand. Before I have a chance to dodge, he swings the glass in a sideways arch, sending ice and glass flying towards me. Dani and Cassie scream in synchronised horror. I wipe my face carefully to check there are no fragments of glass clinging to my skin, but it is only sticky with coke. I see the bouncers out of the corner of my eye and know that all I have to do is remain calm for a few seconds longer.

'Go home,' I tell him. 'You've had too much to drink. Go home.'

'Call the bouncers,' he sneers, 'Kick me out. But once you get out the club you better watch your back ...' His head falls to his chest. He laughs under his breath. He really is wasted. I gesture to Dani that we're leaving. Walking away is the only option – he's so pissed that he's beyond reason. He'll probably wake up in the morning, puke his guts up and have no recollection of how stupid he was.

Tom turns and holds up his hand up for a high-five.

'I told her. Bitch knows what's good for her.' A boy grabs his arm and pulls him upright.

'Starting on a teacher, man. You are in so much shit.' Tom leans forward, breathing cider breath all over me, but I cut him off: 'Tom, if you start something, I will finish it. Do not start with me.' I turn to go and feel Danielle's hand grasp mine. We walk away together, passing the bouncers on the way out.

'Little shit giving you trouble?' they ask. I nod and point towards Tom. They return the nod, indicating that he will be dealt with, and we escape up the stairs and into the cold night air.

Dani beseeches me to try another club, a bar, a pub, a house party if we can find one. Don't let Tom ruin our night. We can recover, we can still have fun, her and me. She won't get asked for ID, not if I'm with her. We can wait for Melissa and

Olwen, go for a few drinks ... I ignore her pleading and carry on striding in the direction of the taxi rank.

'It was a mistake,' I tell her. 'I shouldn't have come out at all.' All I want to do is go home, back to my safe, empty space.

Dani pole dances against a lamp post, shimmying up and down seductively.

'Dogs have pissed up that,' I tell her. She stamps her foot impetuously.

'My God, Cat, you are so boring! Stop being so bloody miserable all the time and let's try somewhere else! Tom won't be hanging around now.'

'I'm going home.'

'Well I'm not!' she snaps. She glances back over her shoulder, to a group of mostly male smokers standing outside the Glan y Don pub.

'If you won't come out with me, I'll go and meet some new people ...' I reach out and grab her arm.

'Get in the damn car. Like hell you're going into a bar by yourself!' I push her in the direction of the taxi rank. 'You are not spending the night wandering around the town centre on your own.' I open the door of a battered Skoda, drop down into the stained velour seats and shuffle across to make room for Dani.

'North Street, please.' Dani gets in after me, slamming the door shut.

'Not a good evening was it?' asks the driver, glancing in his rear-view mirror with a smile. Dani glares at me with murder in her eyes.

'For Christ's sake Dani!' I explode. 'You are fourteen years old and I am not letting you go clubbing on your own.'

'I'd meet other people,' she says petulantly. 'I've got my phone on me, and a fiver in my bra for emergencies.'

I look out of the window as the taxi driver informs us that most of his Friday night fares should be tucked up in bed.

'What are their parents doing, letting them run wild like that?' he asks. Dani says nothing, and keeps her arms folded petulantly.

It's only a short journey home, and within minutes I am reaching for my dressing gown. I am not going to argue with her tonight, but Dani stamps around the house spitting insults, determined to provoke a row.

'You used to be fun!' she snaps as she changes into her pyjamas. 'Now you're always like you are at school. You *never* do anything *fun*.' Her evening has been ruined and she has to blame someone.

'Dani, I'd never forgive myself if you ended up dumped beneath a pile of bin bags down some alley or got glassed by one of Tom's friends. I know I nag, but I'm trying to take care of you, that's all.'

'You didn't look after me when you left home,' she spits, rolling over so that she is lying on the sofa with her back to me.

That night I lie awake in bed, pondering her last statement. I remember us curled up together, playing Olden Times under our Care Bears duvet because the electricity meter had run out, again. I lie there with tears in my eyes, because she's right – I did leave her. It wasn't my choice, but to seven-year-old Dani it must have seemed as though I'd abandoned her.

I get up and grope my way through the darkness. She's still on the sofa, breathing very lightly, probably not fully asleep.

'Dani?' I whisper.

'Wassup?' she asks, rolling onto her side to look up at me, although it's dark and neither of us can see much at all. I don't switch on the light.

'I'm sorry,' I tell her.

'Don't go all mushy on me, you silly mare,' she replies, throwing back the blanket to make room for me on the sofa. 'We bitch at each another, but we don't mean it. We love each other really. Like Mum and Dad.' Ah, Mum and Dad, the perfect role models – if toxic co-dependency can be considered the highest state of marital bliss. 'We don't need to say sorry to one another. We can argue, like, but I know you've always got my back. And I've always got yours. Sisters forever, right?'

'Right,' I reply. 'Right to the end.' We bump fists and then she throws the cover over me, inviting me to snuggle against her and go to sleep.

'Sistas4eva,' she says happily. 'We should get matching tattoos.'

I draw my legs up and lie squashed alongside her, our cold toes touching under the blankets.

5

Geoffrey leans over his desk and glares at me. He is flanked on either side by Mrs Court and Andrew Watson, chair of the parent governors.

'I think we're dealing with a little more than inappropriate language, Caitlin. You threatened him with physical violence ...'

'Actually, I believe my exact words were ...' Here I glance down at the papers in my lap and begin to read: "Go ahead and hit me, Tom, get yourself expelled, or else fuck off out of my classroom ..." At no point did I actually threaten him with violence. The opposite in fact – he had just threatened to set fire to my house and my car.'

I know that Mrs Court is already on my side. All I have to do is get Andrew Watson on board too. So far he has sat slumped in his chair, arms folded across his chest, showing no sign of bias either way.

'I do accept that my choice of words was inappropriate. Believe me, I deeply regret losing my temper. I felt threatened, I became defensive and said things in the heat of the moment. As soon as I regained control of the situation I apologised to the students ...'

Andrew struggles to stifle a yawn. I teach his daughter, Alex, and I know that he's an A&E doctor who often works nights. He is probably annoyed at being summoned to a meeting when he should be at home in bed.

Mrs Court reaches across the desk and lifts a sheaf of papers.

'Mr Jones, the witness accounts do tend to corroborate Caitlin's version of events. There is no suggestion at all that she assaulted or threatened to assault Tom. What we are looking at here is a case of verbal abuse and inappropriate behaviour, not physical assault.'

'I think I've heard enough.' All three of us swivel in our chairs, looking to Andrew. 'We're going round in circles here.' He looks at me, sternly, and I feel like a gladiator waiting to see whether the Emperor's thumb is upturned or jabbed downwards. 'Miss Bennett knows her choice of language was ill-judged, she apologised, and I don't believe for a second that she intended to hurt the lad. If somebody threatened to assault me and damage my property, my reaction might very well be the same as hers. Now, from what Alex says, she's a good teacher and a valuable asset to the school. She's expressed remorse, she's learnt her lesson and I don't believe it will happen again. Let's give her a yellow card and get her back in the game. We've wasted enough time and spent enough on supply teachers in her absence.'

'I agree,' Mrs Court chips in. 'Caitlin is making progress in classroom management. I see no reason to exclude her any longer.'

Geoffrey leans back in his chair and tries to disguise his annoyance as gracious resignation. He has been outnumbered. With poor grace he concurs – I am to be allowed back into Cymraeg 2. However, each week I will have a one-to-one meeting to review my progress and lesson observations with Mrs Court. I'm her problem from now on. That's his way of dealing with problems – that's why he's called Geoffrey the Teflon Headmaster.

If the reward and sanction system doesn't have the required effect, it must be because the teacher failed to implement it correctly. If exam results are poor, it's because the children's primary education was clearly inadequate. And if I go back to work and cause more problems, it will reflect badly on Mrs Court, because she's my line manager. He gives the impression that the whole school is engaged in a conspiracy to undermine him. The school is a collective of failures, and he is the glittering cherry on top of the turd.

Outside in the corridor, I thank Andrew for my second chance. He nods curtly and heads off in search of the exit, probably to sleep. Mrs Court grips my shoulder, and we freeze, wait until he has vanished through the double swinging doors at the end of the corridor, and then, we dance. We hug one another and impulsively I plant a kiss on her cheek. She is my guardian angel, or the closest thing I have to one.

Celebration over, I suddenly become apprehensive. I know that the game has moved up a gear. She is my guarantor, she vouched for me and has taken responsibility for my development. If I get into another confrontation it's her neck, her career on the line as well as my own. You can almost see the newspaper headline: SENIOR STAFF FAILED TO PROTECT STUDENTS IN ASSAULT CASE. Geoffrey would have us both out on our arses.

I can't afford a single slip-up, and I know that the kids will push me even harder now that they've seen my temper. It's not going to be an easy ride.

'Why don't you use the rest of today to get back up to speed?' Mrs Court suggests, steering me towards the staffroom. I'm grateful to her for stepping into the room with me. She stops in the doorway, one hand on my shoulder. Because she's a deputy head, naturally, all eyes turn towards her.

'Good news,' she chirps, 'Geoffrey has reinstated Caitlin to her position in the Welsh department, as we all knew he would. She's starting back with us tomorrow.' There are a few pleased nods and smiles from the ladies of the English department.

From behind his copy of *The Times*, Trevor Oare growls, 'Storm in a bloody teacup. We've all had our moments. Now get back to work.' He lowers the paper and pretends to glare at me, but his furrowed face cracks into a rare smile. At this, the staffroom turns in on itself once again, and I am indeed a storm in a teacup. I am nowhere near as important as the new GCSE grading system or the week's STAR targets.

Cathy Art brings over a cup of mint tea, after absently-mindedly fishing the tea bag out with one of the pencils she keeps pushed through her top-knot. If you met her in a supermarket you'd know she's an art teacher just by looking at her: the asymmetrical hemlines and floaty scarves, the hair in a messy bun adorned with pencils, and the acrylic paint darkening her nails.

'Glad to have you back,' she smiles.

'Hear, hear!' says Baldy Pearson loudly from across the table. 'We couldn't understand why Geoffrey was pratting about prolonging your exclusion.'

'I know!' Milton Shiavone chips in from across the room. 'When I had to restrain that lad last year and his mam accused me of beating him up, the investigation was done and dusted in a few days.'

'Perhaps the Head doesn't like me,' I say. 'Or perhaps he's onto me. He's found out about my plan to oust him and run the place myself.' Mrs Court and I exchange glances, but it's such a ludicrous prospect that the others all laugh.

'It's because you're a woman,' says Vicky Lee, so earnestly that everybody stops laughing and looks at her. 'He's a disgusting old misogynist. How the hell he hasn't been sacked yet, I don't know.'

'Don't sugar coat it, Vicky, tell us exactly what you think!' says Baldy Pearson cheerfully.

'It's all right for you, you're a DWEM. He likes you …'

'This is uncalled for, Ms Lee,' says Mrs Court, quietly but firmly. Vicky turns to look at her.

'It's true, though. He has his favourites, and it's no coincidence that they're all male …'

'Vicky, there's a time to discuss such concerns, and I feel it would be better to have this conversation in private.'

'It won't make any difference,' she says to Mrs Court, before pushing back her chair and gathering up her teacher's planner in a way that makes her ill-humour totally obvious. Before she leaves she turns to me and says, 'This isn't over, trust me. Watch yourself around him.'

The mood in the staffroom has soured. I stay long enough to wait for the kettle to boil, make a quick cuppa, and then I head back to my classroom to see what sort of state it has been left in.

My entire stationary supply has mysteriously vanished. Cathy brings me whatever she can spare from her art supply cupboard. A few window blinds have been ripped down, there are six new gobs of chewing gum trodden into the carpet and ink balls spattering the ceiling. Considering my predecessor came back from a stress-related leave of absence to find the words FAT BITCH carved into her desk, the damage isn't bad at all. The place looks like a shit hole, but the damage wasn't malicious. Small mercies, and all that.

6

I'm a little nervous as I resume my place in front of the whiteboard, but my first lesson is a success. By the time it's over any nervous feelings have been supplanted by ones of frustration. I'm annoyed at having missed over a week's worth of lessons with my classes, because I know I'll never be able to recoup those hours. Supply teachers change with every lesson, and most of the time all they are do is the legal minimum they are required to do – they supervise pupils and stop them from climbing the walls. St. Luke's is notorious for being a difficult school to teach at, but it frustrates me when I see how little effort appears to have been made at actual teaching.

7B have been set 'copy from the whiteboard in silence' tasks. Most of them seem to have taken five minutes to jot down the paragraph about hobbies, and then spent the remaining fifty drawing patterns around the edges of the page. What the hell is that going to teach them?

At least Year 7 have evidence of work in their books. Many books have pages ripped out – used as spit balls perhaps. I doubt some of the supply teachers got beyond copying the tasks onto the whiteboard. I worry my classes will be hoping for another lazy lesson, so I go in determined to get them engaged and back on track. I put on my 'no messing' face as I step in front of the whiteboard, but there's no need to worry. Incredibly, 10J are glad to have me back: 'We had Mr Grimshaw all last week, miss, and he just yelled at all us lesson. WILL YOU BE QUIET! WILL YOU BE QUIET! I even got yelled at for saying "Ow" when Jonas stabbed me with a biro!' Tony Grimshaw is Old School. He's one of the few teachers who can still subdue a class. Shout until they're quiet. Everything is fine, as long as silence reigns. Rumour has it that the Head won't let him retire as they'll have no one to do the announcements on Sports Day.

Damien in my Year 8 Additional Needs class gives me a cheeky wink as he saunters out of class. 'I'll beat Tom up for you next time, miss. Don't want youse losing your job, do we?'

'I didn't beat Tom up, Damien, so there can't be a next time.'

'You should've beat him up. He's got the sort of face that asks for a smack.' Damien continually reminds me of a fortysomething man about town, dispensing a wisdom that belies his thirteen-year-old face. He'll bring sweets to every lesson, and each time I ask him to put them back in his bag, he waves them temptingly under my nose.

'Go on, miss. You have one. We'll all have one. Make our day a little sweeter.' He's a little bugger, but a charmer too, just like his dad – Mr Williams of the soulful eyes, who at parents' evening has a habit of leaning towards you and touching your arm as though he just can't help himself: 'You've done such a wonderful job with Damien. He thinks the world of you, Miss Bennett …' If I met him in a bar and didn't happen to teach his son I'd certainly be interested; but the last thing I need is to tangle myself further in the incestuous web of St. Luke's.

My serious Year 9 class indicate that they're glad to see me back by sitting up straighter and laying out more coloured gel pens than ever before on their desks. They are a perfectly polite bunch, respectful and all a little shy – I guess their parents must have drummed some good old fashioned 'respect your elders' into their heads. Their earnestness sometimes unnerves me. I was never in the top sets.

The only lesson I'm really dreading is the last one, because I'll have to face my GCSE class, and that means coming face to face with Tom Jones. I'm ready to have the Head sitting in the back of the classroom to conduct his observation like a pedagogical Simon Cowell, but it does seem unfair that he's to judge me on this, my first lesson since the incident with Tom. Let me get this awkward lesson out of the way, let me try to re-establish some sort of relationship with 11Y. Let us find a way to move forward together, and then he can observe me as many times as he wants. But his presence will affect the pupils, it will tip the playing field against me and alter the dynamic of the classroom. Geoffrey still believes me to be totally at fault for the incident, and they will pick up on this and play the victims.

Sometimes, of course, it works the other way. My university tutor was a shrewish bully of a woman. When she came to observe me teach she had a habit of singling out children for questioning or snatching their books from under their noses. 'You, boy, what has Miss Bennett taught you this week?'

Seeing that she was looking to criticise the lesson, the class hated her as I did, and without a word spoken they sided with me. Having exemplary pupils made it easier for me to be an exemplary teacher. In the end, the only criticism she could level at me was that I didn't remind students to stow their bags under the desk to avoid a tripping hazard. For one day we had a common enemy, and the honour of the school to uphold. The next week of course, they were back to being little shits.

Now the situation is about to be reversed. Geoffrey will sit on the back row, and the contempt oozing out of him will spread to the students and diminish my chances of earning back their respect.

I'm not religious, but I find myself praying to whomever may be listening – let the Head get locked in a store cupboard, let him slip on some wet leaves or spilled orange juice. I don't want him to be hurt, at least not badly. I just want him to miss my lesson with 11Y.

Suddenly, like a sunbeam bursting through the window, Mrs Court appears in the doorway with her clipboard.

'It's me!' she sings. 'The Head wanted to come and conduct this observation himself, but he's been called away on urgent business.'

I can't hide my relief. 'Do send him my regards when you next see him,' I say, and we both suppress a smile at the mention of 'urgent business.' It's an open secret that if the Head is in an 'urgent, confidential meeting' he's usually porking the secretary. It's been going on for years, but since they are both single, there's no scandal beyond unauthorised use of a school desk. Shudder.

I stand in the doorway and wait for 11Y to arrive. Shoulders back, deep breath.

'Don't worry,' says Mrs Court, 'we've not seen hide nor hair of Thomas all week. That should make things a little easier for you.'

I admit 11Y into the room and go to the front of the class. I manage to keep my voice calm, although my hands are shaking and my legs seem to have turned to jelly.

'*Diolch 11Y. Eisteddwch, os gwelwch yn dda.*' They sit in silence, unnerving silence. Never before have they listened this intently. 'I'm aware that last lesson some of the things I said were inappropriate, and I would like to apologise to you all again for any offence I caused. But I'm hoping that you won't throw away your chances of passing your GCSEs just because your teacher was a complete idiot. What I said was wrong, I don't try and make excuses for it. But I want you to understand why I get frustrated.'

I look out of the window, across the playing fields and towards the red-bricked council estate which engulfs the school. The view from the other window is an industrial estate, stretching down to the banks of the river Dee. It's a place of grim, grey, single-storied units. It's where some of these students will end up, stuffing wet-wipes into packets or putting frozen ready meals into boxes.

'In a few months you'll leave school. Whether you're going into higher education or into employment, you need to do everything you can to boost your chances of getting a job. Even basic Welsh will be an advantage if you work in customer services or the public sector. If I get frustrated it's because I care very much about your success; and I know that you could all pass your Welsh GCSE and get decent grades with a bit of effort. I'd like us to start again with a renewed effort. I'll work at my people skills, if you'll work at Welsh. Can we try that?' Almost in unison, 11Y reach into their bags and take out their Welsh books and writing implements. I take it as a resounding 'Yes'.

'Right, let's get cracking. Nia, hand the textbooks out, please. We'll go to the revision module and see how much we remember from previous lessons, and we'll take it from there.' The mood is starting to lift and a positive energy fills the room. I'm pleased that so much of what we covered in previous lessons seems to have stuck. In spite of their behaviour, it seems as though most of them were learning something, after all.

Only Cassie sits like a little rain cloud in the corner. Probably she's anxious about Tom being missing, so I don't try too hard to draw her into the lesson. The revision goes well, and I decide to move on and concentrate on expanding oral answers. Then, just as we're tackling adjectives and adverbs, the Head enters the room without knocking.

Tom is standing behind him. His left eye badly bruised, so badly in fact, that his eye has closed into a slit. I freeze mid-sentence, gripped by a sudden sickness. Was he suspended for his behaviour, and did his father do that to him?

I manage to stutter, '*Prynhawn da, Prifathro.*' I gesture for the pupils to rise to their feet, but their eyes are on Tom's face, and only a few of them remember to do so. Mrs Court's face has blanched too.

'*Prynhawn da …*'

'Sit.' He silences them with a motion of his arm. He is looking at me. 'Come with me, Miss Bennett.'

'Can I set a task the pupils can complete while I'm absent?'

'No.' The tone of his voice is incredulous. 'Gather up your possessions and come with me at once. You will not be returning to this lesson.' He's furious. How dare I? How dare I stand there and pretend I've done nothing wrong?

I look at Tom's face. He looks away, as though afraid to make eye contact with the big, mean teacher.

'You don't think I had anything to do with this?' I gesture to Tom's injuries.

'Gather your belongings and come with me, Miss Bennett.' He does. He thinks that I punched Tom and gave him a black eye, then had the audacity to come back into the classroom and pretend that I care about my pupils.

I hear myself gasping, 'You don't think I did that … I know I lost my temper but I would never, never …'

'This is not the time for discussion. Come to my office.'

'But I didn't do it!' I shriek.

Mrs Court is on her feet, hand outstretched, placating. 'I think you'd better do as he asks, Miss Bennett. If you're innocent …'

The indignant teenager rears her head. I am not accepting a dressing down for a crime I absolutely did not commit.

'I am innocent! Tom tried to start a fight with me. He threw a drink at me! I walked away. We went straight home. It couldn't have been me.' I'm shaking, I'm sick with disbelief and indignation. How can Tom just stand there and smirk, smirk, smirk? Doesn't he realise what he's doing to me? Doesn't he realise that he'll destroy my career? I turn to him, trying to speak directly to any spark of honest goodness that may lurk beneath his twisted, malicious smile. 'Tell them the truth. Please Tom, if you keep lying you could ruin my career. I didn't do it! You know I didn't!'

Tom turns away, so that he's facing into the corridor. Cassie looks down at her desk, biting her lip. The Head steps forward and takes my arm.

'That's enough shouting, Miss Bennett. Come with me.' I jerk my arm away.

'Tom! You can't do this! You know I didn't touch you!' The Head grabs my arm again, more forcefully this time. He is manhandling me, an arm around my shoulder to propel me towards the door. I stumble against a table, dragged by the collar like a growling dog. Instinctively I put my hands against his shoulders and shove him away from me.

'Get your hands off me!' There is no way the push could have hurt him, but he recoils as though slapped.

'Mrs Court, phone the police. We're now dealing with two cases of assault.' His voice is cold, stern and controlled, like a politician or a policeman delivering bad news. He's rehearsed this moment, planned it all. It's quite clear to me that he's relishing this.

'The police!' Mary cries. 'She didn't do nothing.'

Mrs Court comes to the front of the classroom, her voice almost a whisper.

'Headmaster, I think the situation is getting out of hand ...'

'Phone the police, Mrs Court.' He turns his back on her dismissively. I've hurt his pride, his dignity. I challenged the alpha dog, and that's something he's not going to let go. He has to be seen to win. He jabs a finger in my face.

'You're done. I'll see to it that you never work in education again. You're a thug, an immoral, nasty ...'

'Headmaster!' Mrs Court cries out, stopping him mid-sentence. He turns, looks over the pupils with vague disgust. You can read it on his face – what, you're trying to shield them from my bad language; these pure, poor, sensitive darlings? He's enjoying my comeuppance. I'd put money on him having stage-managed the entire confrontation, the prick. Any normal teacher would have removed me quietly between lessons, and I would have gone quietly. Why now? Is it so necessary to humiliate me?

'Come with me please, Caitlin.' Mrs Court reaches out and takes my hand. 'Come with me,' she says, and I go, trying not to look at my students' faces as I leave the room.

I follow Mrs Court into her lavender office. I'm a curious mixture of trembling anxiety and desk-thumping rage. I pinch the flesh on my upper arms.

'I said things I shouldn't have to Tom. But I never laid a finger on him. I'm a lot of things, but I'm not a liar. I swear that I've done nothing to hurt him.' Mrs Court looks at me for a long moment, like a mother looking for fibs. I hold her gaze, hoping that she'll see the truth in my eyes.

'I know you didn't do it,' she says. 'You've never been a liar. But it's not that simple, Caitlin, you know that. We have to follow procedure.'

She reaches for a box of tissues, not to offer to me, but to dab at her own eyes. One dab and the tissue is discarded. She's my friend, my mentor, and she will always try to make sure I'm treated fairly. However, I also know that she will have to put her loyalties aside and act in the best interests of the school. She's senior management and I've become a liability. In her situation I'd automatically think of the students' safety too. It's what any good teacher would do.

'I'm afraid, Caitlin, that I'm going to have to summon the police, in accordance with the headmaster's wishes.' He's standing in the corridor, looking at me through the wire-set glass as though I'm a dangerous beast. He will tell the police that he was afraid to confront me again. Mrs Court is standing between me and the door, and I know that she is keeping me here for my own safety.

7

Mrs Court walks with me down to the reception, and we sit in the mock leather chairs by the main entrance. It takes half an hour for the police to arrive. They seem unusually kind to me, almost grateful that I'm willing to go quietly. They even wait until I'm sitting in the patrol car before handcuffing me. There are no cat calls from students, nobody bangs on the school windows at the sight of the patrol car in the car park. The officers' kindness and politeness lull me into a false sense of calm, and for a brief few minutes I stare out of the car window as though I'm in the back of a taxi. However, as soon as I try to get out of the police car my legs go weak again. The police woman puts a supportive hand under my elbow and I feel myself involuntarily resisting her, leaning my weight back and dragging my feet like an unwilling toddler. The moment I'm led into the custody suite and come face to face with the duty sergeant my unnatural, zen-like calmness is destroyed by a sudden gut-churning feeling of dread, vicious as a punch to the stomach. I feel like a sheep led by its handlers into the abattoir; a sheep who followed trustingly but now finds its exit barred.

I barely hear a word of what is said to me, but I somehow mumble the correct responses. I'm forced to hand over all my possessions, including my shoes. There's something especially ignominious about being stripped of your shoes.

They lead me to a cell. I hear the heavy iron door slam behind me and the key being turned in the lock. It's only then that the injustice of the situation really hits home. I think of Tom's smirking and Geoffrey trying to drag me out of the classroom, and the anger erupts inside my chest with renewed fury. For a few seconds I lose control and begin to scream and hammer on the door and to kick it with my bare feet. I have no idea what I'm screaming, but the word 'fuck' seems to feature quite heavily.

Someone on the other side of the door opens the hatch and orders me to calm down. I look down at my feet and realise that my toes are hurting. An hour ago I was teaching GCSE Welsh, and now I'm standing in a cell which looks and smells like a public toilet. How the hell did this happen? I walked away from the conflict, I signed up for the therapy, I apologised to the pupils, and I didn't, most definitely didn't hit Tom. I walked away from him … so why is this happening? I made a mistake, but surely I don't deserve to be locked away, to lose my career, for a crime I didn't commit? Thank you, God, so bloody much for screwing me over time and time again. You can stick your Daily Act of Collective Worship and when ESTYN comes to do an inspection I'll tell them that I don't adhere to school policy because God threw me under the bus once too often … But of course, there won't be an inspection, because after this no school will employ me ever again. Fuck.

I don't cope well with being falsely accused of something. When Dad's lying defence barrister said that I was 'frequently physically aggressive' and that Dad accidentally injured me when attempting restraint, I flipped out in the courtroom and screamed, 'I hope horses eat your bollocks, you lying tosspot!' Which I personally thought was quite eloquent given that I was angry enough to start throwing punches. (The judge didn't agree.)

Soon after that I was referred to a counsellor for my first bout of anger management therapy. I was raw as fresh sunburn and every gentle touch felt like a slap. Even as I slept, I dreamt angry dreams. I started to dream about digging a deep grave on the school playing field. Every night I was surprised when Dad blindsided me and I was the one who ended up in the coffin, buried to the sound of my parents' laughter.

I was sent to anger management by the children's home,

after I got caught threatening to hold someone's head under the hot water geyser for stealing the last rich tea biscuit. Looking back, it probably wasn't the threat so much as the fact that I'd got the snack-stealing bitch by the hair and was dragging her towards the sink.

My first counsellor's name was Karen. Whenever I got the urge to yank someone's hair out by the roots, she taught me to take a deep breath and assess the facts of the matter. We started small, with the biscuit situation. It was an over-reaction to get worked up over a biscuit – after all, I couldn't claim ownership of a biscuit which was kept in a shared container. Scalding someone wasn't going to solve the situation, just as screaming and shouting wouldn't make more confectionary appear. There were also ginger nut creams in the biscuit barrel. Were biscuits the problem? Was I really so desperate for a rich tea, or was I looking for an excuse to vent feelings of a more general frustration? (In that instance, biscuits did happen to be the problem. Ginger nuts are disgusting. But I took her point on board about the overreaction.)

I've accepted that I'm an angry person. Like a smoker craves a fag, like an alcoholic needs the bottle, I seem to fight a constant battle against the urge to scream 'FUCK!' and break stuff. Some people are addicted to drink, drugs, sex, gambling, food. I am addicted to the cathartic rush that comes from fighting back, from telling some obnoxious prick to STFU, OMG just STFU.

In order to become a teacher I had to learn to control my temper, and up until recently I thought that I had largely 'conquered' my anger issues. I wouldn't have gone back into the classroom unless I truly believed that I'd be able to keep my rage in check. Thanks to counselling and self-help, I've made real progress since being taken into care.

When my knobhead university housemate drunkenly tried to make pasta at 3am and burnt our worktops, I resisted the urge to beat him senseless with the offending saucepan. When my tweedy bastard tutor groped my arse during the department's Christmas party, I forced myself to step back and wag a playful finger at him. People in the job centre treating me as though I'm dross, those self-service counters in supermarkets, teenage lads wolf-whistling and yelling 'get your tits out' ... I swallowed my rage, counted to ten and kept my cool.

Today though, trapped in the police cell, I realise that I should have jabbed Geoffrey the Teflon Twat in the eye. I should have burnt Knob Head's prized Xbox on a bonfire in the back yard and taught him what it felt like to watch £300 go up in smoke. I should have allowed myself the satisfaction of breaking Gropey McHanderson's wandering fingers. I should have told my job centre 'advisor' that the pittance he doled out wasn't worth the indignity of being patronised by a jumped-up little prick like him.

I should have done all of this and enjoyed it, because ultimately, trying to be good and respectable and responsible has got me nowhere. I lose my temper once, just once; but because of that one outburst I made a mortal enemy of Tom, and suddenly I'm Livia, the Child Catcher and Godzilla combined. My clean record is fucked, my career is fucked, my employability is fucked and I'm stuck in a police cell with aching toes.

8

My toes continue to hurt, but eventually the anger begins to fade. The time for emotion is done. As I'm sitting on my plastic mattress massaging my cold feet I hear Karen's voice calmly telling me: 'Don't give me feelings, Caitlin. Give me facts.'

This is the time to plan what I intend to do. I must be as cold and bare as an empty refrigerator. I close my eyes and imagine myself pushing the negativity to one side, giving me a clean surface on which to place my facts. A refrigerator door will do nicely. The facts, when laid out, are:

1. I got into a verbal confrontation with a student.
2. Said student was suspended twice during the last academic year for fighting on school property.
3. The student now appears to have been physically assaulted.
4. I have been arrested on suspicion of the assault.
5. BUT I have an alibi for the evening of the assault: Danielle.
6. The bouncers saw me walk away.
7. I am innocent unless proven guilty.

Put like that, things don't seem quite as bleak as they did an hour ago. At the moment the police have no *proof* that I attacked Tom. They have only his word against mine. I need to make my words count. I need to be calm. I need to be in control. Most importantly, I need to stop kicking heavy doors with my bare feet.

I remain impassive during the interview with the police. I won't say 'no comment', because that makes me sound as though I have something to hide. They ask me how much I'd drunk that evening, and raise their eyebrows disbelievingly when I tell them that I was stone cold sober because I was chaperoning my teenage sister to an alcohol-free under 18s gig.

It's easy to stay calm at first, because I have Dani as my trump card. Dani is my alibi, and once they've spoken to her they will have to drop all charges and let me go.

Then, the police tell me that five teenagers have come forward to testify that I attacked Tom around the back of the nightclub. They claim that they saw me punching him repeatedly in the face. I grab at the base of my chair and squeeze the seat tightly.

'You've got it wrong,' I tell them. I keep calm and maintain that there was simply no way I could have assaulted Tom; but I don't think they believe what I'm saying.

'Are you telling us all five witnesses are lying?' they ask, with obvious impatience.

'Yes. My version of events is correct, so they must be lying.' But I bet they're used to hearing, 'Honest guvnor, I'm innocent!' from everybody they interview. I bet they deal with compulsive liars and sociopaths every day of the week.

They fire question after question at me, hoping that I'll crack and blurt out an admission – I lost my temper, I didn't mean to hit him, it was self-defence, I was drunk. A guilty plea with extenuating circumstances would be easiest for them. I admit my mistake, no need for a trial and I am punished with the minimum of work on their part.

The 'stuck record' is a useful technique when dealing with argumentative students. I never thought it would work with the police. I keep repeating the same story over and over again. There are no inconsistencies in my story, and it cannot fail to tally with Danielle's version of events. There will be no CCTV footage of the attack. Aside from these 'witnesses', the police have nothing. We go over and over and over my version of events, and I give them nothing. The case will have to go to trial. Finally, they release me on bail.

In the custody suite my shoes are returned to me, but my house and car keys, my mobile phone and my purse are all inside my handbag, which of course, is at school.

'Don't suppose you could lend me a fiver to pay for the bus home?' I ask the desk sergeant, smiling so I look as though I'm joking. Five pounds? Sure. In fact, why doesn't she just phone a patrol car and have them escort me to my front door? I want to tell her that sarcasm is not becoming in a public servant.

It's a three-mile walk home, wearing a thin blouse and not very practical shoes. By the time I arrive back on my doorstep I'm numb with cold and my socks are stuck to my blistered feet. There is just enough daylight for me to scrabble around in the window box and find the spare key hidden in the soil. I get inside, fall face down onto my bed and lie there with my eyes closed tightly. I lie with my face pressed into the duvet, listening to the sound of my breathing, until I fall asleep.

When I wake up it's dark, but I know that there is somebody inside the house with me because I can hear them on the landing, breathing hoarsely.

'Who's there?' I call out in my gruffest voice, instinctively grabbing the copy of *Crime and Punishment* I keep as reading material when I need help getting to sleep. It's a hardback copy, and properly handled could knock an intruder unconscious. Dani appears in the doorway.

'You okay, sis?' she asks softly. 'You left the key in the front door.' She tosses my keys and my handbag onto the bed. 'Mrs Court will drop your car off tomorrow. She says she hopes you're okay. She'll phone you soon.' Dani reaches out and squeezes my arm. 'I've brought you what I made in home ec for tea. It's in the oven. Get something hot down you, have a soak in the bath. I've put the immersion heater on for you. It's bloody freezing in here.' She gives me a brave smile and hands me my dressing gown.

'They think I'm lying, Dani,' I tell her, clutching the gown to my middle like a teddy bear. 'They have witnesses against me; five people who said they saw me hitting Tom.'

'Two versus six,' she replies with a toss of her hair. 'We can take them.'

As we're sitting on the bed formulating our battle plan, her mobile rings and HOME flashes on the screen. I hear Dad's voice distorted by the receiver and am ashamed that I feel a cold stab of fear in my innards. It takes me a second to realise that I'm not afraid for my own sake, but for Dani's. I can hear his agitation, but she holds her own in the face of his disapproval by snapping at him, 'Jeez, take a chill pill, Dad! All I'm doing is checking that Cat's okay. It's not a crime to visit her, is it?' I'm shocked by her flippancy, and tell her that I don't want her to visit me if it means trouble once she goes home.

'I'm not scared of him,' she replies, rolling her eyes.

'Neither was I. Look how that ended.' It frightens me when I see a flash of myself in Dani, because it was a similar episode of foot-stamping, sarcastic petulance that earned me my first slapped cheek. Dad used his open palms to try and subdue me, to cow me back into meek silence, just like he did with Mum. But being a mouthy little fraggle, I refused to be subdued, and Dad upped the ante accordingly.

I tell Dani that I'm grateful for her support, but I don't want her to risk her own safety by provoking him. She, however, doesn't seem at all fazed by the prospect of going home to him.

'He can't keep me locked up. No matter what he says, I'll still come and see you.' I don't doubt her sincerity, but I know Dad and the lengths he will go to exert his control. That's why I'm worried for us both.

9

I know that I'm not allowed anywhere near St. Luke's. Even so, a week after Dani's disappearance I find myself parked down one of the side streets near the school, my hair hidden under a beanie and some large, dark sunglasses shielding the top half of my face. I sit in my car and pretend to be engrossed in my phone, waiting until the 3.30 bell rings and the school empties. I've parked my car down one of the streets I think Dani is likely to walk along to get home.

I don't see her that first day. The second day I don a hoodie and repeat the exercise, choosing a busier route. This time the car is swamped by bodies in red sweaters, and I sink down into my seat, dreading being recognised by any of the students.

Eventually, to my relief, I see her walking with her friends. I wait until she turns the corner, then I follow Dani's footsteps, drive right past her and park up at the far end of the road, knowing that she will have to walk past my car in a few moments. I take out my phone again, keeping an eye on her through the rear view mirror. She is talking to her friend Jess, and neither of them are in any hurry to go home. I chew my thumb nail impatiently. Come on Dani, come on! I can't risk approaching her with Jess still hanging around. Then, just as they seem to be bidding one another goodbye, I look up and see my mum standing there.

It's been years since I saw her, and the sight of her sends a jolt right through me. Her face has sagged. She has jowls and bags under her eyes. She's wearing unbranded navy joggers, a baggy striped sweatshirt and moccasin slippers. It looks as though she's just dragged herself out of bed.

Dani waves farewell to Jess and walks over to Mum. As she does she passes my car, and I'm pretty sure that she recognises me. She gives me the quickest of glances, but is smart enough not to betray me. Mum puts a protective arm around her daughter's shoulders. Dani is fourteen, nearly fifteen; too old to need escorting home. I know then that Mum and Dad have rumbled me. They know that I won't dare approach Dani while she's within spitting distance of the school. They've guessed that I'm going to try and speak to her during the walk home, and they've foiled me by meeting her first.

It's as I suspected: they are behind this. They are keeping Dani from me so that she won't be able to testify in court. She has vanished from Instagram, WhatsApp and Snapchat. I've been blocked from her Facebook account. If I ring her phone I get a recorded message about the number being no longer available.

They are preventing me from contacting her, and in doing so they are taking away my alibi. They want me to go to prison. Whether they are motivated by fear of getting on the wrong side of Tom's dad, or just sheer malice, I can't say.

I park on the main road and walk the short distance to Mum and Dad's. I can see from the top of the road that Dad's car isn't in the driveway. Given that he was always too lazy or drunk to walk even a short distance, this makes it highly likely that he's out of the house.

I pull the hood of my sweater up to hide my face and walk briskly down the street and up the pathway of my old home. I knock loudly, and wait. There is movement on the other side of the door, but no one comes to answer it. Stepping back, I look up at the bedroom windows. Someone, definitely a female, ducks out of view. They are hiding from me. Well, I didn't come this far just to walk away. I kneel, slide my fingers under the flap of the letter box and bring my mouth close to the slot. I speak loudly to make sure my words will be heard on the landing, where I'm sure they are hiding out of sight.

'I know you're in there,' I call into the empty hallway, 'and I want you to listen to me: I didn't hurt Tom. I don't deserve to go to prison for a crime I didn't commit. I don't know why you're doing this, but if you've got even a shred of decency, you'll make sure that Dani's able to speak in my defence. Just let her speak. Let her tell the truth. You owe me that much.'

I get to my feet. I'm aware that several neighbours are out in their gardens, listening to my words. A few glance away or dash indoors, but one or two of them make eye contact, not bothering to hide their curiosity. I don't care. I'm not the one in the wrong here, I have nothing to be ashamed of. I've done all I can do, now it's up to Mum's conscience.

As I walk back towards my car I hear the pounding of feet on concrete. Even before I turn my head, I know what is coming.

'It's Bennett the bitch!' What follows next is hard to describe, but it feels as though I've been tossed into a washing machine on a spin cycle. I am surrounded and jostled by a group of teens. Someone grabs at my hair, another hand whacks me across the bridge of my nose, and finally I'm shoved into the embrace of a privet hedge. They are gone before I can see their faces. It's a pretty ineffectual attack, but it does leave me disorientated. I retain sufficient control of myself to suppress a string of swear words, but as I pick myself up they deliver the *coup de gras*: they return and shower me with a hail of missiles. Most of them are pebbles, but some of them are not. A largish lump of concrete catches me on the cheek, and an empty glass bottle bounces off my temple. I shield my face, expecting another barrage, but they run leaving behind only their shrill, catty laughter.

'Oi! Little buggers!' Somebody is at my side. I cover my eyes with my hand. It's not the injury that draws tears, but the humiliation of knowing that I've just been attacked by a gang of thirteen-year-olds.

'Are you okay?' asks my would-be defender.

'Give me a second,' I reply, furiously mopping at my

eyes with my sleeve. I dry my eyes and find myself looking up at a man a fair few years older than me, his dark eyes framed by crow's feet. His blue-black hair is beginning to grey at the temples. I guess he's mid-thirties, about a decade or so older than me. He's wearing a khaki T-shirt that is a little too tight, showing off his pecs, but also the slightest beginnings of a paunch above his belt. He's very good looking in a whiskery, imperfectly bed-headed sort of way, and I don't mind admitting that for a second I forget the pain in my face and my pelvic floor gives an involuntary twitch.

'Are you badly hurt?' he asks. I shake my head. The lump of concrete caught me square on the cheekbone. It throbs and it will be sore tomorrow, but I've been punched in the face enough times to realise that this is nothing to worry about.

He looks around for the gang. 'Little bitches, what the hell are they playing at? I saw which school uniform they were wearing, if you want to go to the police …' I shake my head again. 'The school then. Complain to the school …'

'There's no point,' I tell him. 'Nothing will be done.' Even if I'd been able to identify any of them, Geoffrey wouldn't lift a finger to help, and the police would start asking questions about why I was in such close proximity to the school while on suspension.

'How are you going to get home? Can I escort you back to your car? Get you a taxi?' There's no sign of the gang, but I let him walk with me back towards the main road. I reach for my keys and realise that my hands are trembling. This annoys me. Compared to the beatings I've been dealt in the past, this is a mere scratch. Why I am so upset by a gaggle of teenagers shoving me into a hedge? He looks down and sees the keys jangling between my fingers.

'I think this has shaken you up a bit more than you realise,' he says gently. 'You look as though you could use a drink.' He glances over his shoulder, in the direction of the Fox and

Hounds pub on the corner. I avoid olde tyme pubs like the plague as they tend to smell of beer and piss, and so remind me of Dad. He must see my distaste, because he quickly changes direction and points to Snax café. 'A cuppa. Let me buy you a cuppa. Don't drive while you're still upset.'

A few minutes later I'm squeezing myself into a yellow Formica booth while he orders two milky coffees at the counter. He returns with two overflowing cups, a digestive placed decoratively on each saucer in place of a biscotti. Clearly, the Italian coffee revolution has bypassed Snax. Still, the cup is huge, and rather ironically for something chock-full of caffeine, it does seem to steady my nerves. After a few gulps I find I can look my champion in the face again.

'I'm sorry, I don't believe we've been introduced,' I say a little too formally, holding out my hand for him to shake. 'I'm Caitlin.'

'Chris,' he says, his smile showing perfectly white teeth. We sit in awkward silence for a few moments, before he asks, 'Do you have any idea why those kids went for you? If it's an unprovoked attack, I really think you should go to the police ...'

'I probably used to teach them. I worked at St. Luke's. I mean, I do still work there ... just not at the moment ... it's complicated.' I reach for a teaspoon and stir my coffee vigorously, even though it doesn't need stirring. Chris bows his head slightly so that his gaze meets mine.

'I think I know who you are,' he says quietly. 'You're that lass ... the female teacher who's been suspended?'

'What makes you think that?' I ask defensively.

'Just a guess. I saw something in the local paper. Female teacher in her twenties suspended from St. Luke's; you saying you work there but not at the moment ... I'm sorry if I've put two and two together and made ten.'

'No, you're right,' I say, my shoulders slumping. 'I have been suspended from work. But for the record, I definitely am not guilty.'

'If that's what you say, I believe you.' I look up at him, surprised. He continues, 'I believe in giving people the benefit of the doubt. There's always three sides to every story, as my old man would say: your side, my side and the truth. I'm not one of these 'no smoke without fire' types, because I know what it's like to have your name blackened unfairly.' He calls the waitress over and orders us another cup of coffee. Clearly he's in no rush to be off anywhere, quite the opposite, as it turns out. For the next ten minutes I find out everything about his divorce from his cheating wife, and although I tend to take pretty much everything with a pinch of salt, I do find myself empathising with him. If even half of what he says is true then he's had a really hard time of it. If it's all true then the man deserves the Nobel Peace Prize.

I'm quite happy to sit there listening to him, nodding along and gazing into his eyes. I don't think he minds me drinking him in along with my coffee, because I can see it's a relief for him to have someone to listen. He's one of life's ranters, like me. We aren't to be confused with talkative or lonely people, like the sort who sit next to you on the bus, make a comment about the weather and then end up giving you chapter and verse on their cat's hysterectomy. Ranters are often quiet, buttoned-up people who seem calm, but are just very adept at hiding their emotions. We tend to prefer baring our souls to strangers and then walking away, temporarily relieved of our emotional burdens. If we are Catholic then we are probably the sort who seek refuge in the confessional; but we are also adept at sensing a fellow ranter who might be happy to lend an impartial ear to our woes. I seem to attract quite a few of them on parents' evenings, and they inevitably overrun their ten-minute slot. It's quite awkward dealing with them when you're against the clock, but I'm quite happy to be a temporary release for Chris.

'She left me for another bloke, but she acts as though I'm in the wrong. She stops me from seeing my girls. She's reported me to Social Services three times, for supposed neglect. They have to investigate every accusation, and I've been cleared every time. She does it to make life difficult for me. She posts all over Facebook about me being an abusive, deadbeat dad who's under investigation, ignoring the fact that I drive five hours to see them, and that I've been cleared of every allegation she's ever made against me. But women see and hear these rumours and run a mile, because as a decent parent you wouldn't put your kids at risk by dating an alleged child abuser, would you?'

'Well, I don't have any kids, so you don't need to worry about scaring me off,' I reply. As soon as the words are out of my mouth I realise that it sounds as though I'm asking for a date. Suddenly, the dregs of coffee in the bottom of my cup become very interesting indeed. I can actually feel myself blushing. It is not a pleasant sensation.

'I have scared a few women off, or rather my ex-wife has. As soon as I start seeing somebody else, the anonymous messages start arriving. She wants to stop me from finding anybody. So, believe me, I know the damage false allegations can do. Innocent till proven guilty, I truly believe that. Get to know a person before you judge them.' He sounds defensive, perhaps realising he's revealed more than he intended to. He pushes his cup away as though ending the conversation. 'There. I've laid it on the table. If you never want to see me again, I'll totally understand.'

'Can I get you anything else?' The waitress asks uninvitingly. Perhaps she's overhead snippets of our conversation, because the look she gives us isn't the friendliest. I shake my head and she waddles back to the counter with a scowl on her face. I look Chris straight in the eyes.

'To be frank, I'm surprised you're still sitting opposite an accused child-beater.' There, give the nosy cow something really juicy to chew on. 'Since the story made the papers I've not had a single message or phone call from anybody other than my line manager. Seems as though everyone wants to believe the worst of me.'

'We're a good match then,' he says, holding his cup aloft. 'To being a black sheep.' I return his toast by clinking my cup against his.

'An innocent black sheep, mind you.'

He smiles apologetically. 'Listen, I'm sorry for going on like this. I'm not normally so bitter. It's just that I drove down to Birmingham over the weekend to spend time with the kids, and she slammed the door in my face. I had to speak to my girls through the bloody letter box ...'

'Been there, done the whole shouting through the letter box thing ... Don't worry about it. You need to unload sometimes, I understand.' From the wry smile he's desperately trying to supress, I'm worried that 'unload' may be construed as sexual innuendo.

We become aware of the waitress hovering over us, cleaning cloth in hand. We've been sitting here nursing the dregs of our cold coffees, trying to postpone the end of the conversation. Chris looks regretfully at his watch.

'I suppose we should be going,' he says.

'I suppose we should.'

'Listen, I know you've got a lot on your plate at the moment, with the court case ... And I've got a lot going on with trying to sort out regular access to the girls, and with working shifts and stuff ... But if you'd like to meet up for a chat sometime, maybe another drink ... a sort of black sheep support network ...'

'I'd like that,' I say, a tad too eagerly. 'As long as you're aware I might be going away shortly.'

'Like I said, I'm not in the position to commit to anything much myself. The girls come first, and until I get something sorted out I'm going to be sort of busy, but if you'd like to meet up sometime …'

We exchange numbers and I add it to my pathetically short address book: Danielle, Dentist, Doctor, Fenella, and Work.

'We'll definitely keep in touch,' I say, as we exit the café. 'And perhaps in six months' time we'll have come through all of this and we'll be able to talk about something other than how shit the past few years have been for us both.'

He waits for me to get into my car, gives me a smile, a little salute and saunters off with his hands in his pockets. I look into the rear-view mirror to watch him walking away.

I catch sight of my own reflection in the mirror, and suddenly, I hate my own face. I hate that I still look and feel like a victim, even after all these years. I hate the fact that my life revolves around work, or not being able to work. I hate that I only have a sense of purpose when I'm Miss Bennett, and that Caitlin is little more than a sad sack who has no Facebook friends, no real friends for that matter. I've pushed people away due to my own insecurities and issues, and now my best friends are my line manager and my fourteen-year-old sister. When your most meaningful interaction consists of using the self-service checkout or telling a telephone scammer to go to hell, you know that your life badly needs an overhaul. Something tells me that it would be a big mistake to let Chris become one of those 'friends' I never actually see.

Before I know it, I have jumped out of the car and am jogging down the street after Chris. I shout his name. I see his green T-shirt vanish behind a bus shelter and I shout a little louder, not caring if I sound desperate.

'Chris!' He stops and turns. I run towards him.

'Caitlin! Are you okay?' he asks, concerned. I'm a little breathless as I pant, 'Can we start again?' He looks at me quizzically. 'Can we forget all we've just told one another? Can we stop being the black sheep?' I often forget to modulate my voice, the result of months of fighting to make my voice heard at back of a noisy classroom, and the words seem to boom out of my mouth. An old man at the bus shelter turns and stares at us, presumably confused by my ovine reference. Chris hesitates, and in that moment my heart lurches into my stomach. Then he holds out his hand.

'I'm Chris,' he says. I take his hand and shake it, a smile of relief blooming on my mouth. He understands what I mean. 'I'm unmarried and a proud dad of two little girls.'

'I'm Caitlin,' I reply. 'I'm twenty-four, and I'm a Welsh teacher.'

'I'm an engineer on the offshore wind farm. I'm also a reserve firefighter.' A man in uniform who isn't going to slap handcuffs on me. Today just got a quite a bit better.

10

Later that week I go to the magistrates' court to answer the charge of assault with a plea of not guilty. It's a formality, over in minutes. I don't hear from the police again, but clearly they decide that they have enough 'evidence' to proceed, because the next thing I know, I'm informed that a trial date is set for three weeks' time.

Not wanting to risk another ambush, I write a letter informing Mum and Dani of the trial date and post it to them via Royal Mail. I find myself checking my phone compulsively, hoping for a text or WhatsApp from Dani. Each day, as the trial grows closer, I find myself growing a little more despondent. Neither the letter box plea nor my letter had any effect.

In the week leading up to the trial I am contacted by several journalists wanting my side of the story. I'm a bit surprised at this, as our local papers seem to depend upon Twitter for newsgathering, but it seems as though there are still some journalists still willing to graft the old-fashioned way and piss people off by banging on their front door.

Having shooed off a number of reporters, I have become wary of answering the door. I pre-empt their questions by sticking a note in the side window:

I AM INNOCENT. NO FURTHER COMMENT.
PLEASE GO AWAY.

It seems to do the trick, until the Wednesday before the court case. I'm upstairs when someone knocks on the door. I don't bother to make my way downstairs, having no intention of answering them; but this person knocks and knocks and knocks until I realise that they won't take no for an answer. I throw open the door, ready to give them a mouthful of abuse.

Mum is standing on my doorstep. She is on her tiptoes, desperate to step over the threshold. She doesn't want to be seen visiting me. In she comes, her eyes sweeping the room furtively.

'This is a nice place you've got here,' she says, seating herself on the edge of the sofa. I sit on the big chair opposite her, noticing how ridiculously small and bird-like she has become. She was always on the unhealthy side of thin, but her arms and ankles look almost brittle. She's always had a downturned mouth, but age and gravity are not being kind to her face. She resembles an anorexic bulldog, if you can imagine that.

I don't offer her coffee or tea. She fiddles with the sleeves of her knitted sweater as though waiting for a cue to speak. She looks back down at the coffee table and pulls lint off her cuffs. The silence between us grows denser and denser. She flicks a bit of fluff onto the carpet. Its whiteness annoys me. Finally, she speaks.

'Friday morning I'll bring Dani over to you. I'm supposed to be taking her to school, so she'll be in her uniform.'

'Thank you.'

'Your Dad won't be happy that we've gone behind his back. You'll have to protect her.' I open my mouth to point out that as her mother, surely she has some duty to protect her daughter? But then I remember all the times she must have heard Dad hitting me and never intervened. Why expect her to change the habit of a lifetime?

'Of course I'll look after Danielle,' I snap. She has the decency to look embarrassed.

'I'm sorry it's taken me so long to come and see you. I couldn't open the door the other day ... neighbours gossiping, y'know, it might get back to your father. But she'll be there, I promise. I hope she's able to get you off the hook.' She looks at me, a faint, pleading smile on her face. Her eyes are like discs of lapis lazuli. But she's a stranger to me now. I barely recognise anything of myself in her. 'I know you're innocent,' she says. 'You were always hot-tempered, but you aren't malicious. Not like that.'

'Frankly I'm surprised you can remember me,' I say. 'What's it been, six years?' Stop it, Caitlin, I scold myself. What are you hoping to achieve by raking over the past like this? She's here to help – take it and let her go back to living her own pathetic life.

'I did what I thought was best,' she replies, her voice quivering. 'I'm sorry if it didn't seem that way, at the time. I couldn't tell you the truth back then ... I don't know if it will do any good to you to hear it now ... but it can't harm you either ...' Spit it out, woman. Stop talking in riddles.

'I presume you're talking about Dad?'

'Yeah.' She takes a deep breath, steels herself. 'There's a reason why he treated you as he did ...'

'I've always wondered what I did to deserve it.'

She raises her thumb to her mouth and bites down on her nail.

'You didn't do anything. But I did.' Silence. In that heartbeat's length of a pause I know what she's going to say, I suddenly know why he hates us both. The only thing that surprises me is that I didn't realise it long, long ago.

'He's not your dad.' Like a game of Tetris, all the pieces suddenly fall into place and everything explodes.

'So, who is he then, my real dad? You can't drop this bomb on me and give me half the story! I want to know who my biological father is.' Biological, as though I was grown in a laboratory like a germ, or sprouted off a hairy tomato plant in some greenhouse like a freak.

She shakes her head and whispers, 'I can't. I'm sorry.'

'Why can't you? Too many to choose from? You were too drunk to remember? You never found out his name?'

'I wish I could tell you, but I can't. That's all I can say. I'm so sorry.'

'Why tell me then?' I croak. 'How did you think this could possibly help me? Or is it just about making yourself feel less guilty?' She mops at her mottled cheek with the palm of her hand.

'You're right, I made a mistake. I've made so many ... I've let you down ... I'm not a proper mum to you, or to Dani. I'm absolutely pathetic, I know that ...' I brace myself for the outburst; but she takes a deep breath, clasps her hands between her thighs and although she rocks backwards and forwards, she seems to have calmed herself. 'I'm not going to subject Dani to what I put you through. I'm done with hiding away ... Oh God, my life is such a mess ...' Her self-composure vanishes as she dissolves into sobs. Pitiful though she is, with tears pouring down her cheeks and self-recriminations pouring out of her mouth, I remain on my chair with my arms folded. Once again, it's all about her. She's not sorry about what happened to me. She doesn't care what's happening to me right now. She just wants to unburden herself and make her misery somebody else's problem.

When I don't rush to comfort her she gulps back her tears, managing to restrain herself again.

'I'm nearly forty, Cat. Forty and I've wasted my whole life being afraid. But I'm not afraid anymore. I'm done. I'm out.' I've heard this before. A hundred times she screamed at Dad to get out. A hundred times he shouted at her, 'Why don't you just leave if I'm such a waste of space?' The truth is that she's not strong enough to live without him. She's a teenage mum who never managed to grow up and be a parent. She is utterly pathetic.

'I'm glad you've found some form of closure. Thank you for bringing Dani over next Monday. Now, go back home and please don't worry about me.' I sound cold and imperious – a

Victorian mother trying to bully a daughter into making a loveless marriage. Mum looks up at me, startled by my tone. 'What? You've unburdened yourself, got rid of your guilty conscience, you've talked about your problems – that's why you came here, isn't it?'

'I came because I'm your mother.'

'No, you're not. There were a hundred times when I needed a mum, and where were you? Where were you when Dad was dragging me out to the garage by my hair? When he got so drunk that he knocked me unconscious and broke my bones … where were you? Hiding from him! Where were you when I was in hospital, in a children's home? Too busy wallowing in your own fucking misery.' I know I'm about to lose it, but I can't stop the words coming out of my mouth. Years and years of animosity come pouring out of me like sick, and I can't help myself, can't silence myself. It's cathartic to pour it all out and lay my hatred at her feet. 'You knew he hated me, but you did nothing to stop him. You put your own children in harm's way. But what really hurts me is that you had a chance to start again. He was in prison for months. We could have gone to a refuge, moved away, just us girls. I would have forgiven you for being pathetic and neglectful. But you didn't …' My voice cracks involuntarily. 'I waited for you, in hospital. I wanted you to stand next to me in the witness box.' I pause, press my hand to my mouth, furious at myself for crying. 'But you walked away, and I can't forgive that.'

I wait for her to start crying again, wait for the resurgence of self-pity and the hysterical breast-beating that any sort of confrontation would provoke. Instead, she stares at me.

'You've wanted to say that for a while, and I've wanted to hear it. I'm glad to get everything out in the open, at last. I was scared of him, too scared to leave. He would have found us, Caitlin. He told me so many times that he would kill me if I left. I had to let you go.'

She gets up from the sofa and perches on the arm of my chair, holds out her arms like a baby reaching for its mother. In spite of my anger, something stirs inside of me. I hold her, for the first time in half a decade, and feel her whole body convulsing with silent pain. She leans her head on my shoulder, pressing her cheek into my collarbone. I can see that her roots are growing out. Not yet forty, and her hair is salt and pepper. Life is killing her faster than it kills most people.

'I don't want your forgiveness,' she murmurs. I bite my lip hard. 'Oh my baby girl, my baby girl, I don't care if you hate me, but I need you to know how much I love you. I know I'm sick and weak and useless. I'm sorry I was a bad Mum. I'm sorry … I'm sorry for everything.' We hold each other until her sobs abate, and all I can hear is the ticking of the clock in the kitchen. She wipes away her tears and takes my face in her clammy hands.

'You are my brave, beautiful girl. I'm sorry I have to leave you.' She's going back to him, as she always does, like a junkie needing a fix. 'I hope your court case goes well.' The tears are drying and her mouth is fixed into a gently determined smile. 'Remember, whatever happens, you and Danielle will always be there for one another; and I'll always be watching over you.'

No, you won't, I think, as she closes the front door gently after herself. Even now you're turning your back on me.

11

The next morning I phone my solicitor with the news that I now have a witness. I see this as reason to celebrate. He is more cautious, and takes this as an opportunity to warn me that I will be painted as the blackest of black by the prosecution. I will have to try my very best to stay calm during the trial. They claim to have witnesses and medical reports saying Tom was punched repeatedly, leaving him with a fractured eye socket. If the magistrates disbelieve Dani and I'm found guilty, then the severity of the assault means that I will almost certainly be sent to prison.

'I'll be blunt,' he tells me. 'Whether or not you did it, if you would plead guilty they'll go easier on you. Your sentence automatically gets cut. You won't keep your job, but they would probably give you a suspended sentence. It's not too late to change your plea. And it might be best if we keep you from having to testify in court.'

I know he's right. There's a certain hardness about me that nothing seems to soften. I won't be easy to defend, but I can't plead guilty just to avoid a jail sentence. For the past six years everything I've done has been geared towards getting me into the classroom. I have no other ambition, no other experience to draw upon, no plan B. I need to stay in teaching, and that means the magistrates *have* to accept that I'm totally innocent. It's all or nothing. Death or glory.

When the solicitor realises that I'm going to listen to him, he advises me to make preparations. 'There's not much else we can do except turn up on the day, present our best argument, present your witness, and hope. But don't worry, you're still in a magistrate's court and even if you're convicted, six months is the most they can give you.' He doesn't seem to understand that I'm not fazed by the prospect of going to prison. Violence and confinement don't scare me as they do most people. I know that the real punishment begins once you're released, with an eviction notice looming and a criminal record on your CV.

Following that morale-boosting chat, I head over to Andrea's office for what may possibly be my last counselling session. It's a shame, because over the past few weeks I think we've built up a decent rapport. I still don't talk about my parents, and Andrea doesn't ask about them. Since we established that ground rule we get along just fine.

'The court case is tomorrow, isn't it?' she asks. I nod and stare out of the window at the concrete Buddha in her little courtyard. I don't really feel like talking about tomorrow. I've set up direct debits to cover bills, informed my landlord and handed a few things to Mrs Court for safe keeping. I've done all I'm able to do. Talking about it won't achieve anything.

'Perhaps we could discuss some coping strategies, just in case you do find yourself sent to prison?' Andrea suggests. I bite back a smile, because an image pops into my head of Andrea brandishing a shiv. She appears to have read my mind. 'I have worked with ex-offenders,' she says, a touch defensively. 'I do have some idea of what prison life is like.'

'I don't doubt it. But truthfully, I'm not that worried. If someone starts on me, I'm confident that I can handle myself.'

Now it's her turn to suppress a smile. I'm five foot two and weigh nine stone. I don't exactly look like the sort of person who'd have the upper hand in a physical confrontation – but appearances can be deceptive.

I've been getting into fist fights since I turned thirteen. Growing up, I had only two choices: be a victim or be a bitch. There were girls at the bus stop who would spit on you just for walking past them. They'd trip you up, follow you home, throw Coke cans at your head, shout that you were a slaggy little *cont* (one of the few bits of Welsh they'd bothered to learn), call your mum a psycho and your dad a piss head.

It wasn't gang culture or anything. We didn't carry weapons or have particular allegiances. They were just bitches who were unhappy with their own lives, but were too stupid to do anything constructive about it.

After years of Dad drunkenly smacking me around, I wasn't scared of anybody. I got in a few cat fights with the girls, and I always won. I learnt one of the most basic classroom management lessons in the car park behind the Spar shop: choose your battles carefully. You can't fight against a whole group and win. Take down the leader, and the rest will usually leave you alone.

Second rule is that you can never back down. Never let them see your fear, or sense your weakness. Tom's late brother started going out with one of the bus stop bitches, and challenged me to a fight to 'defend her honour'. I made things worse by telling him that she'd lost any honour she may have had in the back of a Ford Fiesta. After that I had to agree to the fight, although Dani cried and begged me not to. I went down to the Rec Ground fully expecting to have my face rearranged, but as we were squaring up to one another he backed out. We shook hands and he acknowledged me as a 'tough little nut', and nobody gave me any shit after that.

By the time I was fifteen I was pretty much bulletproof: 'Caitlin Bennett, she's a real bitch.' They may have meant it as an insult, but it also conferred a certain status. It wasn't so much an adjective as a rank. You don't mess with a bitch. You don't like her, but you leave her alone, because a bitch will always fight back. I'm not physically stronger or braver than anyone else, but I developed a reputation for tenacity, and that's why the bullies gave up and left me alone. That, and the fact that I'm willing to fight dirty.

I know I can handle myself in tough situations, but I also know that getting beaten up hurts. I'd rather avoid getting my head kicked in, if at all possible. I make a promise to Andrea:

'If anybody gives me any trouble I'll try an assertive coping strategy before breaking their nose, okay? And I promise to do my mindfulness exercises each night as I'm lying in my bunk ...'

'Using humour is a good coping strategy in itself,' she says. I'm deadly serious, but I return her smile and don't say anything, just in case by some miracle I get through this unscathed and am in a position to return to work. I don't want her writing *possible violent/ psychotic tendencies* on my employment record.

'Is there anything else you'd like to talk about?' she asks, and I surprise myself by answering, 'Mum came to see me yesterday. First time in over six years. First time we've spoken since I was taken into care ... or rather, since she gave me up.' Andrea nods her head slightly to show that she's listening carefully. 'She came to tell me that she'd arrange for my sister to be a witness at my court case ... Oh, and also that I'm a bastard. My father isn't my biological father.'

'And how does that make you feel?' I hesitate, because truthfully, up until now I've not really given it too much thought. To be fair, I've had other more immediate things to worry about.

'Relieved, I suppose, that we don't share the same DNA. Frustrated too, because Mum won't tell me who my real father is. I'm not sure she even knows herself. It's thrown up a lot of questions that probably won't ever get answered. On the other hand, I suppose it explains quite a few things ...' I shrug. 'I'm just throwing adjectives at you. I don't really know what I feel.'

'And your mother ... May I ask about her?'

'You can ask, but I haven't really got an answer.'

Andrea nods again. 'It's a lot to take in, especially when you have more pressing matters demanding your attention. Just be aware that a delayed emotional response may happen at a later time.' I find myself wondering if Dad ever felt any kind of delayed regret for what he did to me. I doubt it. You have to be a hard-faced bastard to break your daughter's ribs in a drunken rage, and then stand up in the dock and claim self-defence.

At the end of the session Andrea gets to her feet and offers me a hand to shake. 'I hope to see you next week,' she says. 'Whatever happens, do keep in touch. I'm here if you need to talk.'

'Let's hope they have phones in prison.'

'Don't give up hope,' she urges, and then gives me a surprisingly comforting hug.

Chris phones as I'm driving home from therapy. 'Listen, I'm sure you're busy, this may be really bad timing on my part … but I'm off work today and I'm not on call … If you're free at some point and would like someone to take your mind off things … perhaps we could meet up? If you're in the mood to see anybody else, that is?' The prospect of returning to my empty house does not fill me with glee, so without hesitation I tell him, 'I'd like that very much. How about you pick me up in half an hour?'

He phones a taxi and takes me out to a country house for lunch. He absolutely insists that he'll be picking up the tab. He's celebrating handing in his notice at work, as he's accepted a role as a full-time firefighter. It's an extravagant lunch as he insists on three courses for lunch, and a glass of champagne with the meal. We drink to his new role, and then he offers up a toast, 'To justice'.

We walk home along the country lanes, hand in hand. We stop at every pub we come to and sit in the beer gardens so that I can see the trees and flowers, and enjoy the spring sunshine. I've never been one for nature. I'll go outside when required to, but rambling, gardening, birdwatching or any kind of planned outdoor activity holds little appeal for me. Today though, it's different. I'm busy making memories, which I will hoard in case I find myself boxed in by grey concrete walls.

I can't remember what we talk about as we stroll – I only remember that I laugh more than I have done in years. For minutes at a time he succeeds in making the sick feeling in the pit of my stomach go away. He makes me forget about what I'll have to face tomorrow.

Eventually, we end up back at mine. Chris kisses me shyly on the doorstep, and it's dizzying. I haven't felt this way about a man since I looked up at the stage and saw Rhys playing bass. The moment our eyes first met was like eating sparklers, but kissing Chris is a whole mouthful of Catherine wheels.

I grab his hand and pull him into the living room. I've not had sex for years, and I'm aware that this may be my last opportunity for a few months. I make the most of it, crying out loudly enough that the neighbours bang on the party wall. I laugh. What are they going to do, call the police on me?

At 5am Chris slides his arm around my waist and kisses the back of my neck. He has to go, has to catch the boat out to the wind turbines before the tide turns. I lie in bed, listening to him shower, then at the last moment I spring out of bed and join him in the bath. One last time, to make up for all those weekends spent planning lessons, marking, catching up on sleep … I didn't know what I was missing.

He gets dressed, makes me a cup of tea, kisses me goodbye.

'I'll hope to hear from you tonight,' he says.

'If you don't, you'll read it in the papers. But I'll phone you as soon as I'm able to.'

'I'll visit you.'

'No, you won't.'

He leaves. I tie my damp hair in a turban and crawl back under the duvet while it retains the scent of his aftershave and sweat. I order myself to get a few hours' more shut-eye. There's a strong possibility that tonight will find me in a new bed, and if so, I doubt I'll be able to sleep soundly.

12

I wake to find that Dani has let herself in using the spare key. She has removed her tie and sweatshirt, and is busy ironing my best blouse on the kitchen table. There's a sausage sandwich and a pot of coffee waiting for me.

She smiles at me bravely, but her face is so pale that the shadows under her eyes look like bruises. I throw my arms around her and hold her as tightly as I can.

'What if I get things wrong, Cat?' she asks, her voice quivering.

'Tell the truth and you can't go wrong,' I tell her. I'm aware, for the first time, of the enormous burden I'm putting on her shoulders. 'Sisters forever, Dani, right to the end, no matter what happens today.'

'My God, Cat, you are so ...' Her fingers make a square shape to indicate how thoroughly uncool I am. She smiles her sardonic smile, but her mouth is trembling.

I eat my sausage sandwich, head back to the shower to wash my hair and then dress in my best interview suit. Dani continues ironing and packing my clothes into an overnight bag. We spend half an hour going through my wardrobe, picking out what she called a 'capsule closet' of practical, hard-wearing items. I tell her to keep the black stilettos she 'borrowed' from me. Now I sit and watch helplessly as she folds and re-folds the garments, trying to squeeze everything we selected into my holdall. I try to help her, but she waves me away impatiently, trying to hide the tears she's crying into my bundled socks.

At half past eight Mrs Court arrives to take us to court. I hand her a folder containing all the important legal documents in my possession, and spare copies of all my keys. We smile at one another, but we both wordlessly assume that she'll be holding onto them for a while.

She drives us to the court as silently as a chauffeur. As we pull into the car park, Dani reaches out across the seats and grabs my hand. We are greeted by the security guard and the court clerk. We're the first trial of the morning, and are taken through to Court One, where we can sit and watch the others arrive.

Dani and Mrs Court have to sit in the viewing gallery at the back of the room. I hug them both tightly, then go to sit in the dock, next to my solicitor. He shakes my hand and wishes me luck.

'I think you'll need just as much luck as me,' I tell him. 'You're the one who's got to get me out of this mess.'

Tom arrives with his dad. Cassie and her mum arrive moments after them, followed by five more youths who must be the five 'witnesses'. Cassie is the only person I recognise as being actually present that night. The rest of them are strangers – people who owe Tom's family a favour, no doubt.

I only glance at Cassie, not wanting to appear intimidating; but what she does next sends a bolt of nerves to my already unsettled stomach. She looks right at me, her mouth twisting into a funny little smirk, and then turns to Tom and whispers something into his ear. I expect him to look up at me, mirroring her contempt, but his eyes stay firmly on the floor.

The magistrates enter. For some reason I'd expected them to be wearing wigs and gowns, and seeing them in ordinary blouses and shirts makes them a little less intimidating. We all rise as they take their places at the bench. Then, just as the order to be seated comes, a ringtone cuts like chainsaw through the silence of the court.

'Will everybody please ensure that all mobiles phones are turned OFF,' announces the chair, her face almost gargoyle-like in its displeasure. I glance around. Dani's face is scarlet.

She fumbles in her bag, trying to locate her phone and silence the warbling. When she does find the phone, her fingers are trembling so much she can hardly swipe the screen. The call ends and she breathes a sigh of relief.

'Phones off, please,' snaps the court clerk, glaring at my sister. She looks so terrified that I fear she might not be able to take to the stand. Seconds later, the caller tries again and the ringtone resumes. Dani swipes frantically, hopelessly. She is close to tears.

'It's Mum's phone,' she squeaks. 'I borrowed it and the screen's broken and it won't …' The second call ends and she is left frantically pressing buttons. Mrs Court leans over and examines the phone.

'Can you find the off switch?' she asks. Dani presses a button on the side of the phone, but rather than the off switch she is hitting the volume button. I know this because Dani gets another incoming call, and the ringtone sounds like a klaxon.

'OUT!' booms the chair. At her word two things happen: Dani flees, tears racing down her cheeks, but more surprisingly, so does Tom.

'You … you get back here!' his dad bellows, but Tom is hot on Dani's heels and faster than a whippet with a rocket up its backside. The chair looks as though she's about to explode.

'We'll adjourn,' she snaps. Seconds later, Dani's head appears in the doorway and she beckons me, panic-stricken. I jump down from the dock and rush towards her. She holds out Mum's phone. I take it and hold it to my ear.

'Elsa? Is that you?' The fifty-fags-a-day croak on the other end of the line is strangely familiar.

'No, it's her daughter, Caitlin. Who's speaking please?'

'It's Mrs Edwards next door.' I've not lived next door to Mrs Edwards for over half a decade. For someone who used to spend hours peeking through her blinds, her powers of observation obviously aren't what they used to be.

'Mrs Edwards, Elsa gave her phone to Danielle. She's not here at the minute. Can I help?'

'To be honest love, it's you I'm trying to help. There's water coming out of the side of your house. We think there's a leak, or a tap left on.'

'Aren't Mum or Dad there?'

'Your dad's car is gone, and there's no sign of your mam. The doors and windows are all locked and the funny thing is, the spare key's gone and all. If someone can't get here soon I worry the ceiling will fall in ...'

'Thank you, Mrs Edwards, I'll be right there.' I end the call and turn to look at Dani. 'Mum's still at home, isn't she?' Dani nods, dumbly. There's no sign in her face of the panic that I'm currently feeling. Perhaps Mum hasn't tried for years, perhaps I'm over-reacting ... But she was emotionally fragile when she visited me. If she's had a relapse ... I have to check on her. I know from experience that every minute counts.

Mrs Court has stayed inside the courtroom, along with everybody else. I need her car, but I can't risk going back inside and having my exit barred by security ... Just then, the solicitor appears in the doorway and beckons me back to the courtroom.

'Sorry, I've to go somewhere,' I tell him.

'But the chair's already furious ... I can't go back in there and ...'

'You'll have to. Something's come up.'

'Something? What do I tell her?'

'It might be a matter of life and death,' I reply. Dani's eyes widen, but before she can start asking questions I grab her wrist and pull her towards the door. 'Come on, Dani – run!' The solicitor shouts something, perhaps about an adjournment, but I don't hear him; nor do I hear the questions Dani fires at me as we sprint from the courtroom, and within a minute she is too out of breath to run and talk at the same time. As we leg it across the car park I see a commotion out of the corner of my eye – Tom and his dad shouting at one another over the bonnet of a car.

The magistrates' court is about half an hour's walk from Mum and Dad's, or fifteen minutes at a brisk jog. Driven by adrenalin, I push myself to go faster still, until my ribs scream with stitches and my lungs and calf muscles hurt in a way I've not experienced since I gave up cross-country running. Dani lags behind, panting and cursing me. A childhood spent playing knock-door-run serves me well: I know the alleys and the labyrinthine warren of the council estate like the back of my hand. Crossing school playing fields and using the odd back garden as a cut-through, we make it home in under ten minutes. It still might not be fast enough.

I stagger onto the street gasping for air, and find Mrs Jones number 24 and Mrs Edwards standing in the front garden.

'Your Mum's not answering the door, love,' wheezes Mrs Edwards. 'But there's water running indoors …' She points a nicotine-yellowed finger towards the living room window. Still panting and breathless, I cup my hands, place them over my eyes and peer in through the glass, which is thick with salt fret and bird crap. A thin column of water trickles down from the ceiling. Mentally, I try to map the layout of the upper floor. The water is almost certainly coming from the bathtub.

I rattle the front door and give it a quick kick for good measure. Of course, it doesn't budge. Dani is scrabbling about in the earth of the front yard, looking for the spare key stored in an old Eucryl tooth powder tub. She looks up at me, her face ashen. The earth beneath her fingers has recently been turned over, but there is no tub.

'The key's missing,' she says. 'What are we going to do?'

I take a deep breath, and look again at the front door. It's a new one, UPVC with a double-glazed glass panel, designed to be virtually impregnable. All the houses round here had them fitted under a government renovation grant. All the windows too are new, and solid in their frames.

'We need to get in the house. Call the police and an ambulance.' I tell the two women. They gawp at me as it dawns on them that this is something more than a leaky tap. I head around the back of the property. All the curtains, front and back, are drawn. The back garden is heaped with rubbish, and I'm not talking a few old sofas and broken fence panels. There is literally weeks' worth of rubbish spilling out of the horizontal wheelie bin and across the lawn. The door of the garden shed is missing, revealing a three-legged table holding a variety of rust-brown garden and DIY implements. I select the heaviest, a wrench, as my weapon of choice.

At the back of the house is a small lean-to, leading from the kitchen to what was once an outside toilet. Although the back door has been upgraded the fitters seem to have overlooked the lean-to, perhaps classing it as an internal door because it is tucked away beneath a narrow roof. It's a solid wood door, with bolts on the inside, but I'm glad to see that its weak spot is still there. The glass panel is plain single-glazing, bought and improperly fitted by Dad to replace the safety glass he managed to smash after he lost his keys. (He was so drunk it never occurred to him to knock on the door for admittance.) For the first time ever, I'm thankful that my ex-father is a slovenly, maintenance-shy alcoholic.

Dani has followed me round the back of the house.

'Cover your eyes,' I order, pulling the sleeve of my jacket down over my knuckles. I avert my own eyes and swing the wrench against the glass panel. It takes two attempts to shatter it. I knock the rest of the glass through, making it easy for me to reach in and unbolt the door from the inside.

The kitchen is empty.

'Stay here,' I tell my sister.

'But …'

'Stay here!' I bark, going through into the unused dining room-cum-parlour. Nothing. The living room is also empty, but not for long. The carpet underfoot is sodden, the ceiling is bulging and before long the bath will come crashing down.

'Mum?' I shout. No answer. I head upstairs.

Three of the doors on the landing are open. The fourth one is the bathroom, and that, of course, will be locked. Part of me prays wordlessly, prays to whatever unseen being who may perhaps be watching over us; prays that I'll throw open the door and be confronted with clean white tiles and a bare carpet. Let this be a mistake, a misunderstanding.

Dani has come to the foot of the stairs and is staring up at me anxiously. I give the handle a quick, fruitless twist and then take a few steps back. Taking a run up, I kick the door with the flat of my foot, trying to put all my weight behind it. The kick jars my knee and sends me reeling backwards. I'm not going to be able to boot it open like they do in the movies. I grab the handle, push it down firmly and barge it with my shoulder, over and over again. I feel the bolt on the other side begin to give way. I keep going with renewed effort, slamming my entire weight against the wood.

'What's going on?' Dani squeaks. I grunt in reply and keep shoulder barging the door. The lock is stubborn. For what seems like an eternity I'm there slamming my weight against the door. Just as I begin to think that I'll never manage it alone, the lock gives way and I fly through the door and into the bathroom, landing on my knees. The carpet is saturated with water, and is soft and squelchy like moss. Except that it is pink. The water spilling over the edge of the bath is pink.

She meant it this time. She's in the bath, but wearing a T-shirt and shorts. There's a near-empty bottle of vodka on the floor. Her left arm hangs over the side of the tub as though she passed out seconds after discarding the bottle. Blood drips onto the carpet, trickling down over her fingers.

97

She's left-handed, and her right arm has been hacked from the inside of her elbow to her wrist. It bobs on the surface of the water, so that she lies in a pool of her own blood.

I hear myself moan, 'Oh fuck.' The blood is everywhere. It's between her toes and in the grouting. Her hair fans out in the water, its colour changed to that of rust. I touch her neck and feel the faintest pulse. Despite the warmth of the water, her skin is cold to touch. She's not bled out, not yet, but there's gallons and gallons of red water … I reach up and snatch a towel off the hand rail.

'Dani, phone an ambulance!' I shout, pushing the door to, in case she should creep up the stairs and see the bloodbath. 'Tell them to hurry!'

'I'm on the phone to them,' she calls. 'They're asking what's wrong with her?' I hesitate. I don't want to give her nightmares.

'Attempted suicide,' I reply. Dani squeals a high, mournful cry that reminds me of a rabbit I once found after it had been run over. It died squeaking at my feet before I could help it.

I try to push Mum's head back to look inside her mouth, but the shape of the bath means that she slides further down into the water. I jam my fingers between her teeth and feel for bile or vomit. Nothing. She's not choked and her chest is still rising and falling.

'Airways are clear, she has a faint pulse, but she's unconscious,' I call. 'Tell them she's lost a lot of blood and I can't stop the bleeding, Dani, they need to get here fast.' I hear her sobbing, the voice on the phone's loudspeaker staccato and calming.

The deepest cut is on the wrist itself. I lift her right arm out of the water. I can see inside the cut, the flesh beneath the skin. It makes me feel faint. I grab the towel and wrap it around her arm tightly, squeeze and squeeze and squeeze, applying as much pressure as I possibly can.

'Mum, wake up. Talk to me. It's Caitlin, talk to me. You have to wake up. Can you hear me? Mum, don't you do this.

Stay with me. Stay with me. Can you hear Dani downstairs? Stay with us. Don't you dare bleed out. I'm not letting you go.' Already though, blood is soaking through the towel. Where are those paramedics? I let her arm drop and rush into Dani's bedroom. There's a pile of clothes lying at the foot of her bed, and I quickly extract what I need from it and dash back into the bathroom. I loop her hessian cartoon print belt around the fleshy top of Mum's arm and pull as tightly as I can. I've never made a tourniquet before; only seen it done in zombie films when they've had to amputate a bitten victim's limb – but a faint memory of some basic first aid training tells me to hold her arm above her head so that the blood runs back towards the heart. Her head sinks below the water line. With a shudder I plunge my left arm elbow deep into the bloody water and pull the plug. As I raise my arm again the water trickles down the length of it and into my arm pit, covering my best white shirt with red splotches. I want desperately to be sick, but I can't let go of Mum's arm, so all I can do is turn my head to the side and try not to heave. After a minute or so, the bleeding from Mum's arm seems to slow to a trickle.

The sight of so much blood is making me faint, but I force myself to talk to Mum constantly, as though the sound of my voice is the only thing anchoring her to life. I beg her, urge her, order her and threaten her.

Suddenly the paramedics and police are in the room, easing Mum's arm out of my grasp.

'What's her name? How long has she been like this?' The floorboards creak dangerously and a policeman urges moving her as quickly as possible. Within moments they have her out of the bath and are easing the belt off her arm. She is stabilised, wrapped in a foil blanket and placed onto a stretcher. A paramedic with a fauxhawk turns to me and says, 'Good thing you got here when you did.' Then, they are gone. A policeman puts a hand on my shoulder and repeats a question. I hear it, but I can't speak, I can't think.

I get to my feet slowly. My legs are stiff and sore from spending so long on my knees. I push past the policeman and limp after Mum.

The paramedics have negotiated the turn at the bottom of the stairs and are carrying her through the living room. Dani blanches as she sees Mum wheeled out on a stretcher. Then she looks to me, sees the blood, and she screams.

'It's okay Dani, she's alive. They're going to look after her,' I tell her, but looking like a butcher's apprentice, I don't move to comfort her. Mrs Edwards and Mrs Jones will look after Dani. I don't want Mum to wake up alone in hospital.

We leave in a wail of sirens. The paramedics talk kindly to me. I don't hear a word they say, but their voices are gentle and optimistic as though they're putting a sticking plaster on a scraped knee. I guess they're telling me that she's going to be okay, but I look at Mum's face and it is corpse white. How can anyone bleed so much and survive?

We arrive at the hospital and I let go of Mum's hand and watch them wheel her into A&E. I don't try to follow her, but stand there, stupid with shock, until a nurse puts a hand on my shoulder and suggests I might like to wash and have a sit down. I'm led to a toilet marked 'staff only' and offered a clean, coarse towel. I look at myself in the mirror. My shirt, pristine white for court, my hair, my cheek, my arms, hands, trousers, even my socks, are soaking wet and matted with blood. I scrub at my skin, emptying half of the handwash container over my bare arms. There's nothing to be done about my clothes. I look like Bela Lugosi's lovechild.

The nurse is waiting outside. She takes the red splotched towel from me and deftly throws it into a sluice. Then I'm taken to a waiting room, where I'm brought a cup of sweet, milky coffee. She leaves, promising an update soon. I sit nursing my beverage until it turns tepid. The nurses pop in occasionally. They smile kindly, say a doctor will be with me as soon as possible, but hours later I'm still sitting alone with nothing but my thoughts for company.

Mum didn't come to see me to offer support – she was asking for help herself. I should have gone back home with her and packed her bags – but I wanted to get rid of her and dwell on my own problems.

I only saw what I wanted to see: the neglectful mother coming to rain misery and bring me down with her. My mother came to see me for the first time in half a decade, and I acted like a petulant teenager. If she had been a pupil of mine I would have seen beyond my own contempt and realised what she was going to do.

What exactly did she say to me? *But I'm not afraid anymore. I'm done. I'm out … my brave, beautiful girl … I'm sorry I have to leave you … I'll always be watching over you.* Anyone with the vaguest understanding of subtext would have understood what she was planning. How could I be so blind to what was coming? This wasn't a cry for help. She was serious this time. Anyone who can lock the doors, drink the vodka, take a blade to her arms and wait for death like a half-butchered pig doesn't want to be rescued. She'd put a lot of thought into how things would play out after she was gone. She knew that Dani would be in court with me, so she wouldn't come home for lunch as usual. Had I not got there first, Dad or the police would have had to break down the door, and they would have been the ones to discover her.

She didn't want Dani to be the one who found her dead in the bath. She planned this, and I was too dense, too preoccupied to see it. Her visit wasn't an attempt at reconciliation – it was a goodbye. She came to hand over the reins to me, to make sure that Dani had someone other than Dad to care for her. She came to give me the truth, a deathbed confession of sorts, and at the same time, she gave me an excuse to cut Dad irrevocably out of my life. Why didn't I have the foresight to see that she was about to do the same thing herself?

I watch the walls of the waiting room glow yellow in the sunshine, then fade to grey as the sun moves across the sky and the room is cast into shade. Finally, a young Asian doctor comes into the waiting room. He looks exhausted.

'Are you with Elsa Bennett?' he asks, and apologises for keeping me waiting so long.

The doctor asks me about her moods, her usual medication and any possible emotional upsets. He explains that Mum has been stabilised after losing a significant amount of blood. They have pumped her stomach to get rid of the vodka. They estimate that she lost consciousness only a short time before I arrived. They are hopeful that she will recover physically, with no long-term damage to her internal organs.

'Mentally, though, your mother is a very sick woman. We worry that if discharged she will try once more to end her own life. We feel it is in her best interests to section her under the Mental Health Act and transfer her to our psychiatric unit, where the staff will do everything they can to help her.'

He asks me who Mum's nearest relative is.

'I suppose it will have to be me,' I tell him. 'I'm her eldest daughter.' In fact, I'm the only person it could be. No way am I letting Dad near her while she's this vulnerable. He has never taken her suicidal thoughts seriously, dismissing them as a ploy for attention. I've heard him drunkenly goad her on. Dani is too young, and Mum has no real relationship with her own parents. I met my grandparents a handful of times. They stopped sending Christmas cards when Dani was born.

The doctor takes me to an office, where he talks me through Mum's assessment and treatment. He's very thorough in his explanations, I'm clear on the difference between section 4 and 2, next of kin and nearest relative. I'm grateful that he's talked me through the procedure and I know exactly what to expect next, but I'm exhausted by this point and glad when he says, 'I suggest you go home now, and try not to worry. She's in good hands.'

'Can I see her?' He is reluctant, but I persuade him to allow a quick supervised visit, and am shown to a private room at the end of the ward.

'Two minutes,' he says quietly.

She is lying with her back to the door. Her damp blonde hair fans out across the pillow, and clad in the hospital's off-white nighty, she looks like a rebellious angel. I sit on the edge of her bed and take her hand in mine. Both her arms are bandaged. Her eyes are hard like flint, and fixed resolutely on a spot of painted wall. I touch her hand and her fingers are stiff, as though she's determined not to acknowledge me.

There's a lead ball in my throat. It pains me to see her like this: limbs stiff and eyes glassy, like a discarded doll. But I have a lifetime's experience of dealing with pain. I swallow hard, and the knot in my throat sinks down into my middle. It becomes a weight, an anchor, stabilising and making me strong and solid.

When I was afraid and angry, Mrs Court and Marcus believed that I could change my situation for the better. When I was at my lowest, two people told me that I could be strong, independent and smart enough to achieve something. Only two people – but they were enough to make me believe in myself. Perhaps Danielle and I can be enough for Mum. This is her lowest point. The only way to go is up, and I will hold her steady as she climbs.

'Listen to me, Mum: whatever has made you depressed, we're going to confront it. We can't go on like this. I'll look after Dani, but it's only temporary, okay?' I rest my hand on her shoulder and give her the gentlest of shakes. 'Are you listening to me? I love Dani, but I'm not her mother. She needs you.'

Mum closes her eyes and furrows her brow as though the weight of the world is pressing down with invisible fingers and crushing her skull.

'You can get better,' I say, taking her hand firmly in mine and squeezing her fingers. 'You can be strong. I need you to be strong. I've been without a Mum for so long.' In a single blink, her eyes have softened. It's barely perceptible, but I lived with that stone-faced expression for so long that I can see she is actually listening to me.

The doctor moves silently towards me. 'I think your mother needs to rest,' he murmurs. I kiss her on the cheek.

'I'll come and see you whenever it's allowed, and whenever you need me. I'll look after Dani until you're ready to come home.' I don't tell Mum that I'm still facing a possible jail sentence, and that Dani might end up in care or back with Dad. At present she's too fragile to deal with any more guilt.

Out in the corridor I go to a handwashing station and tear towels out of the dispenser. 'I don't know why I feel guilty,' I sob, dabbing at my eyes with the rough green paper. 'She's the one who turned her back on me, but I feel as though I'm the one betraying her.' The doctor takes up a box of tissues and offers them to me.

'Don't feel guilty,' he says gently. 'Depression is an illness, try to understand that her thoughts and behaviour are not rational at present. Many people I've worked with here describe depression as darkness – they don't cease to love the people around them, but they are surrounded by the darkness and can't see a way ahead. They feel as though they are alone in the world, so they stop thinking about the people around them. This is the place she needs to be, so that we can support her and help manage her illness. With your understanding and care, her recovery will be quicker.' But will it be permanent, I want to ask – but I don't.

13

I go outside in search of a taxi rank. There isn't one, but there's a bus station at the far end of the car park ... then I remember that I have no money, and the walk home is impossibly far.

I go back into the warmth of the hospital foyer and walk up and down aimlessly, hoping to see signs for some sort of hospital benevolent fund. You see people being discharged from hospital all the time on TV, and you never wonder how they get home. My life feels like a drama at the moment, except that I don't have the convenient ability to cut between scenes and summon taxis from thin air.

I go to the reception desk and ask if I can use the hospital's phone to call a friend and arrange a lift. The receptionist smiles sympathetically, but says that the line is reserved for incoming calls. She points me in the direction of a pay phone, until I explain that I haven't got any money with me. She must take pity on me, because she fumbles in her desk organiser for a fifty pence piece.

I put the money into the phone, pick up the receiver and try to visualise Mrs Court's phone number, but I'm a digit or two short. Speed dial is a wonderful thing, until you find yourself stuck in a telephone box. I can't afford to dial a wrong number, so hit the reject button and the coin drops into the tray at the bottom of the machine. That's when I hear someone call my name. It's a man's voice, instantly familiar.

'Caitlin Bennett,' he says, sounding relieved. I turn around to see Marcus Williams, my old social worker. Greying at the temples, but otherwise unchanged. 'You're looking a bit lost. Luckily, I've been sent to find you, take you down the police station.' I'm so relieved to see him that I almost throw my arms around his neck, but at the last second I remember my blood-stained clothes and refrain from doing so. 'Your little sister is waiting for you. How's Mam?'

'She'll live,' I say. 'They've sectioned her.'

'She'll get the help she needs. It'll be better for you all, to have her safe in here with doctors and nurses to look after her. You look done in, our kid. I'm sure you'd rather go home, but I'm afraid I'm going to have to ask you to come to the police station with me. Danielle's there, and she's fretting that you've done a runner.' He lowers his voice. 'Like your old man.'

'He's gone?'

'We phoned him earlier. He said it wasn't his problem and hung up. Turned his phone off.'

'Why am I not a bit surprised?'

'Is he still drinking? He sounded drunk on the phone.' We leave the hospital and walk across the enormous car park.

'You'd have to ask Danielle. I've not seen him since he was sent to prison.'

'But you've maintained some sort of relationship with your mam?'

'Not really, no. She called to see me this week. It's the first time we've spoken in about six years. I think she was trying to apologise, make amends. She came to help me sort a problem out; but at the same time I'm pretty sure she was planning this. By helping me stay out of prison she was making sure I'd be there to look after Dani ...' I pause, realising that Marcus must be unaware of my impending trial. The trial, oh hell, I'd forgotten about it until now. Running out of court won't have endeared me to the magistrates, or my solicitor.

I look up at Marcus and take a deep breath, readying myself for a long explanation.

'This morning I was supposed to be standing trial for assault. I ran out of the court room when Dani got a phone call about Mum. The magistrates are going to be so pissed off with me for leaving ...'

'Aye, I heard about your little run-in with Thomas Jones. It was all around the school.' We stop and he unlocks the doors of his Hyundai. 'Saw it in the paper too. The staff and kids are all hoping that you'll get let off. Our Damien thinks the sun shines out of you.'

'Damien?'

'My nephew. My brother Michael's lad. You've met Michael at parents' evening.' Damien, Year 8 special needs. Damien with the never-ending supply of sweets.

'I didn't know he was your nephew.'

'It's a small world. He showed me his school report, I mentioned that I knew you and ever since then I get regular updates about your lessons. He speaks very highly of you, as does his dad. You need to watch our Michael, he's a bit of a charmer.'

'I don't think you need to worry,' I tell him, as we drive out of the hospital car park. 'I won't see him again. I very much doubt I'll be keeping my job at St. Luke's.' I think back to the witnesses, smirking at me from across the courtroom. 'What happens to Danielle if I go to prison? She'll get taken into care too, won't she?' For all her posturing and bravado, Dani is a sensitive soul. She won't cope well with the upheaval.

'Putting her with a foster family is an option, yes,' Marcus replies, 'but hopefully she can stay with her family. She's already indicated that she'd be happiest staying with you.' He slows the car, indicates and pulls to the side of the road. He sits quietly for a moment, gripping the steering wheel tightly, frowning slightly as he thinks. 'Why don't we stop off at the magistrates' court now, and explain the situation?' he suggests. 'I don't know if there's a way we could postpone the trial, but I'm sure they'll appreciate the courtesy of an explanation.'

'Let's do it.' He turns the car around and we double back on ourselves and head towards the court. We park around the back of the building, out of sight of the main entrance.

'You wait here,' he says. 'Can't have you walking into a court looking like that. I'll see if we can take you in via a back door, have a quiet word, okay?'

I may look as though I've stepped out of a slasher flick, but I've spent most of the day stuck indoors, parked on my arse. As soon as Marcus leaves I get out of the car and stretch my arms up to the sky. After the stuffiness and artificial lighting of the hospital the sun on my face is delicious; and with the trial still hanging over my head, this could be my last chance to sunbathe for several months. I lean back against the side of his car and close my eyes. The warmth of the sun-drenched metal through the cotton of my shirt is sheer bliss.

'Miss …' Am I becoming paranoid? Is my overwrought mind playing tricks on me? Tom's family and his 'witnesses' will all be at home by now. 'Miss Bennett …' The words are grunted, quickly and apologetically, as though the speaker is embarrassed. I turn around and look over the top of the car, to see Thomas Jones sitting on the low wall bordering the car park with a tray of chips in his hand.

'What do you want, Tom?' I ask, wearily. His brow narrows in a scowl.

'I was waiting in case you came back. No need to be so snarky.'

'Oh, I do apologise. I'm sorry if I've hurt your feelings by being snarky! You're having a laugh, aren't you? Taking the moral high ground after all you've done, all your lies … Christ on a bike!' I get back into the car, slamming the door shut. I can't deal with him, not now. I need him to take his lies and his imaginary witnesses and piss off to the other side of the moon.

My head is pounding. I close my eyes tightly and hope that he will leave me alone. He taps on the glass. I want to scream at him: leave me the hell alone! Tomorrow you can sneer and gloat all you want, you and your lying bastard friends, when they drag me off to prison and put Dani into care …

Another tap on the glass. I grab the handle and throw the door open, jump out of the car and lunge at him, screaming, 'Fuck off!'

He jumps back, but he doesn't fuck off. He is frozen to the spot, eyes widened, his right hand outstretched from tapping on the glass. I glance down at my bloody clothes. I appear to have genuinely scared the shit out of him. If I wasn't so exhausted, mentally and physically, I could take advantage of his fear by convincing him that I'd carved someone up in a fit of rage, and that he could be next on my list … but right now guile of any sort is beyond me.

'What happened?' he asks. He sounds genuinely curious, almost sympathetic.

'My mum … she …' I shake my head. I can't put it into words. I can't speak, because speech requires thought, and I can't bear to think about those gashes on her arms, meaty tissue visible beneath the trickle of blood; about Dani's unearthly scream or the look on her face as I left her and stepped into the back of the ambulance. If I think about those things I will start to cry, and I am not going to cry in front of someone so determined to see me brought low.

Suddenly I'm feeling lightheaded, as though someone is kneeling on my chest and preventing me from breathing. My legs don't want to hold me up. I take a seat on the low, red brick wall and breathe deeply. I feel as though I want to keel over, sink to the floor and close my eyes. It takes a minute or so for the feeling to pass.

'Are you okay, miss?'

'No, I am not okay. I am very much not okay. I can't talk to you right now.' I grip the wall to steady myself.

'Wanna chip?' I shake my head, but he proffers the tray anyway. 'Maybe you need something to eat,' he suggests. I

109

recognise the gesture as a kind one by someone totally unused to offering emotional support. This is a brief moment of rapprochement, a white flag, a football being kicked across No Man's Land. At this moment in time he is a young man with a tray of chips, and I am a young woman in visible distress, nothing more. It would be churlish not to accept. Plus my stomach is growling with hunger. I reach out and take one.

'Thank you,' I say. Then, I notice something. He is offering the tray with his left hand because his right one is set in plaster. He's tried to hide it beneath a long-sleeved T-shirt and an oversized jacket, but the cast is just visible, peeking out from beneath his sleeve. Somebody has written 'Love' on his plaster knuckles, then crossed it out and replaced it with 'Hate'.

'Your arm ...' Quickly he hides it behind his back. I look up at him. There's no point asking, 'Who did that to you?' I was asked a dozen times by teachers, how did I hurt my shoulder, my wrist, my ankle? Fell down the stairs, getting off a bus, playing hockey ... I always had a plausible excuse on the tip of my tongue. Tom will have one too. He'll lie, like I always did.

'Sit down.' He hesitates, scared of where this is going. 'Sit down,' I growl. He sits at my side, placing the tray of chips between us like a shield. I tell him, 'Somebody fractured your eye socket, and I'm guessing it's the same person who put your arm in that cast. I don't expect you to tell me who did it, but you should tell someone. Whoever they are, stop defending them, stop protecting them. Nobody has the right to abuse you.' He moves a little, a squirm or twitch indicating discomfort. I look him in the eyes. 'That's what it is, Tom. Physical violence is abuse, and it won't magically stop happening. I kept quiet about it. I was ashamed. For years I put up with the beatings, and took my anger out on other people. I let it go on until I ended up in hospital.'

'Was it bad?'

'Fractured ribs, fractured sternum, and a chipped tooth.' I hook a finger under my upper lip and pull upwards to display my left canine, which is a slightly different shade to my other teeth on account of it having been repaired by a dentist. It's pretty crap as far as battle scars go, but I'm not able to show him the real damage, which was all internal. 'He hit my head on the coffee table once. Hit my nose too, but luckily it didn't break.'

'What happened to the guy who attacked you?'

'Ten months jail sentence. Think he served about six.' Tom shakes his head and looks down at his dress shoes, which look to be much too big for him. He probably borrowed them for appearance's sake.

'Was it your dad what did it?'

'Yeah,' I reply.

'He's a bit of a bastard, isn't he?'

'That's a bit of an understatement.' Footsteps on gravel. I look up and see Marcus walking towards us. 'Talk to Mrs Court,' I urge Tom. 'Nobody has the right to hurt you. Remember that.' I get to my feet as Marcus approaches. I say to him, 'One of my students. A well-wisher.' He smiles at Tom, but it's a wary smile.

'The magistrates will see you,' he says quietly. 'But we have to go now, in between cases.' I follow him round the back of the building, where a security guard is waiting at a back door. I step inside, into a dim room which must adjoin the courtroom. The three magistrates are sitting around a square table, drinking tea and looking a little more human than they did this morning.

'I'm sorry I left court without an explanation …' I begin, but the chair gets to her feet and comes over to me.

'Your social worker explained the situation. It must have been a horrible experience for you.' She glances sympathetically at my bloodied clothes. 'I understand you're guardian for your young sister too?' I nod, although I suspect Marcus has been economical with the truth there. 'I'm sure you want to get home, get changed and see your sister. We won't keep you. The trial won't be rescheduled for a few days, I hope that's enough time to sort things. Be sure to inform your solicitor of the developments.' She offers her hand. I clasp it, force a smile and apologise for the disruption. The other two murmur sympathetically.

When we go outside, Tom is gone. Marcus gets behind the wheel of the car, fastens his seatbelt and sighs.

'I might have exaggerated slightly there,' he admits.

'I guessed.'

'Laid it on a bit thick, made out that you were already Danielle's legal guardian. They sometimes let off people who have dependants, give a suspended sentence instead.' He turns to look at me. 'Don't tell my boss I did that.'

I hesitate, but I have to ask, 'How do you know that I didn't hurt Tom?'

'I don't,' he replies. 'But I know that you're pleading not guilty. You've always been a bit volatile, but if you made a mistake you always held your hands up. If you say you didn't do it, I believe you.'

'Thank you,' I say awkwardly. I intend to further prove my innocence by revealing to him that the young man I was talking to was in fact my alleged victim. Would he be within a hundred yards of me, if I'd broken his bones? Instead, I say something far more important, something I've been waiting years to say: 'Thanks for believing in me, Marcus. For everything you've done. I know I gave you a lot of shit over the years.'

'Just doing my job. You don't need to thank me.'

'I do. You turned my life around.' We stop at traffic lights and the car idles in neutral. He twists in his seat to look at me.

'No, Caitlin. You did that all by yourself.'

Car back into first, he turns right and joins the main road. I sit there for a second, my throat tight with emotion.

Then he says, 'Enough touchy-feely crap.' I find myself smiling. Marcus has always 'got' me. Perhaps because of his unorthodox way of handling things, he was the one charged with telling me that Mum had signed me over to Social Services, and that I would be spending the foreseeable future living in a children's home. Wisely, he decided not to tell me in the office. He took me down the bottom of the garden, out of the other children's hearing. As I sat there reeling at my abandonment, he pulled back the branches of a buddleia plant to reveal several wooden packing crates he'd hidden there previously. He handed me a pair of safety goggles and a claw hammer. Those packing crates absorbed my hurt and anger, blow by blow, kick by kick, stamp by stamp. When other kids came to enquire what I was doing, he glibly told them, 'Making a start on bonfire night.' It was July, but they believed him.

Freshly clad in a sweater and jeans, I follow Marcus inside the police station. It's the same station I went to after being arrested for assault, and the same one I attended to press charges against Dad. My stomach tightens into a knot as I'm led past the custody desk and the interview rooms. The WPC behind the desk, the one who made the sarcastic comment about ferrying me home in a patrol car, is now smiling kindly at me. She shows us to a 'family suite', which is very like a prison cell except for the sofa and tea making facilities.

Danielle looks up as she opens the door, and the fear in her face makes my insides ache. Before I can say anything, she has her arms about my neck and is squeezing me so tightly that I fear for my collarbone. Her hair smells like washing up liquid.

'I thought they'd taken you away!' She looks up at me fearfully. 'Mum ... did she ...?'

'No,' I reply. 'She's been sectioned, honey. She'll be in

hospital for a few weeks, but she's going to get the help she needs.' I brush a few tears off Danielle's freckled cheek.

'I don't want to go back to Dad. Can I stay with you, please?' It hurts me that I can't say, 'Yes, of course, you can stay with me forever'. But as Marcus reminded me, I'm not in a position to be making promises. She sees me hesitate, and bursts into tears.

'They won't send you to prison, will they? They can't still put you on trial …' I want to comfort her, but I daren't hope that the meeting with the magistrates will grant me a reprieve. I choose my words carefully: 'It looks as though the trial will go ahead. If I'm found guilty we might have to be apart for a few months. But if I have to go away, I promise that I will come back. If you need me, I'll be there. Always.'

Night has fallen by the time we're allowed home. We fall out of the taxi and through the door, exhausted. I give Dani my debit card and a sheaf of takeaway menus, while I make a few phone calls of my own.

Firstly, I text Mrs Court. She rings me right away, and I ramble on semi-coherently until she tells me, 'It's obviously been a massive shock. I can hear that you're exhausted. Go to bed, try to get some sleep, and I'll call and see you both in the morning.'

Then, I call Chris. 'Good news, eh?' he exclaims happily.

'Not quite,' I reply. He asks whether there's anything he can do to help and offers to come round. Dani is waiting downstairs for me, so I tell him that I'll see him very soon.

I end the call and take a few minutes for myself, sitting cross-legged on the bed with my eyes closed. My stomach thinks that my mouth has gone on strike, and I'm aching all over. I want so much to stuff my face until my stomach groans, then give myself over to the embrace of my duvet and pillows.

But adrenalin is still coursing through my veins and my mind is racing. Sleep will not come easily tonight.

There's a knock on the door – the delivery driver with our takeaway. I go downstairs, clutching the bannister to steady my trembling legs. I hear Dani say, 'You wanna tip? Try delivering the food while it's still hot.' She closes the door in his face. I smile to myself. Where does that swagger and that sass come from? Not from the passive, weak parent we have in common. If I tell her that we are only half-siblings, will it make a difference to our relationship? Is there any point telling her, if I have no idea who my real father is? My mind is racing again, an internet browser with a hundred different tabs open. Any second now I'm going to crash.

'Cat, tea!' Dani shouts.

'Coming now.' I need to reboot, in preparation for tomorrow. It can't possibly be as gruelling or horrible as today, but there's a hundred things to take care of before the trial is rescheduled.

'I got us pizza,' Dani shouts. 'Half 'n' half – pepperoni for me, chicken and bacon for you.' She knows me so well. The table is set the table and she is busy lighting a plate full of tea lights. She looks up at me, smiles.

'Thought we'd play olden tymes again,' she says. I know then that I will never bring up the subject of my paternity. Dad ceased to be my dad six years ago, but Dani will always be my sister.

14

I wake up to the sound of Dani's snores. She is lying next to me curled up like an apostrophe, used to sleeping in a narrow single bed.

The immersion heater hasn't been switched on in twenty-four hours and the tap runs ice cold. My shower will have to wait.

I go downstairs and eat the last slice of pizza, cold from the box. I put the greasy boxes into the black bin, and then sit at the dining table with a pen and paper to make a list:

> Phone solicitor
> Take suit to dry cleaners
> Go food shopping
> Phone Marcus with new trial date
> Phone school re. Dani
> Collect D's belongings

I glance up at the clock: 8.55. Might as well get one job over with by ringing St. Luke's. Lynne, the attendance officer, recognises my voice.

'Caitlin! You got off, then?'

'Trial postponed. Listen, I'm calling about my sister.'

'Your sister?'

'Danielle Bennett, 10Z.'

'I didn't know she was your sister! You don't look much alike, do you?'

'No, luckily for her, we don't. Listen Lynne, our mum was taken to hospital yesterday, so Dani won't be in for the next few days. I'll let you know what's happening as soon as I find out, but you'd better take the number for her social worker, just in case I'm not around.' I give her my mobile number and Marcus's too.

'Good luck, Caitlin,' she tells me. 'I hope you and Danielle get things sorted, and your mum gets well soon.'

The sound of my voice has woken Dani. She's standing at the foot of the stairs, dressed in one of my nighties and rubbing her eyes.

'What's for breakfast?' she asks.

'Whatever we want.'

She goes to the cupboard and opens it. Of course it is empty, because I cleared everything out in anticipation of going to jail.

'Decide what you want and then we can go to the supermarket and buy it.'

'Can I get some clothes?' she asks.

'From the supermarket?'

'From home.'

I remember arriving at the children's home with a bin bag full of clothes, all of them second hand donations. 'Just a temporary measure until we can take you shopping and get you some new things,' I was assured. It was indeed a temporary measure, and I was soon given the promised new wardrobe; but in those first few unsettled days, the contents of the black bin bag just served to compound how profoundly my life had been turned upside down. I didn't even smell like me any more.

Dad isn't at home, and by the look of things he's not even been near the property. The back door is still unsecured. Somebody else has also discovered this point of entry, because the TV, DVD player and other electrical items are missing. I can't catalogue them, but you can see where they once sat, because each stolen item leaves behind it a rectangle of polished wood, highly visible on surfaces thick with grey dust.

The carpet underfoot is still sodden, and more alarmingly, the ceiling bulges. Dani and I skirt around the sagging plaster, our backs to the wall, and tiptoe upstairs.

'Anyone there?' she calls, and I'm relieved when there is no reply. We open the doors as though we're soldiers in an action movie, ready to spring back at the sign of any movement within, but the bedrooms are all empty and untouched. I hand her a few bin bags and tell her to pack quickly.

'School books, too,' I say. She rolls her eyes. I'm being square again.

I go into our parents' room and open the curtains to let in some light. I don't want to chance electrocuting myself by flicking a switch, not with the wiring potentially swamped by water.

Even knowing that the house is empty save for ourselves, I'm still tense. Every creaking floorboard, every car driving past, has me flying to the window to check that there is nobody outside.

'Five minutes, Dani!' I call. Then I roll up my sleeves and begin to pack some of Mum's things. She won't be coming back here. I have no intention of taking responsibility for this place, she can't possibly live in it while it's in its present state, and the task of repairing it will be beyond her. Let Dad sort this mess out, or let it rot.

The floor is a carpet of unwashed clothing. I don't bother trying to sort any of it, grabbing instead the few clean items hanging in the wardrobe. I find a pair of decent shoes, and a few bras in an open drawer. Properly fitting bras are hard to find, so I take her entire stock. I'll buy fresh knickers for her later. Nobody wants to go rummaging through their mother's underwear drawer.

'Dani, we're going!' I shout.

'One minute ...' she calls, dumping a fifth black bag outside her door. Where does she get all these clothes from?

I was lucky to get a Reebok sweatshirt for Christmas. Non-uniform days were a matter of careful outfit rotation.

I grab a few of the bags and head downstairs. As I walk past the sideboard I remember that Mum used to keep important documents in the left-hand drawer. Sure enough, they're still in there: birth certificates and inoculation certificates, a few of our early hand-drawn Christmas cards. I have a copy of my birth certificate somewhere at home, but now I'm holding the original in my hands. It's yellowed and creased, and sure enough, the space for the father's name is left blank. I remember asking Mum about it many years ago, and her telling me, 'Your dad was at work when I took you to be registered. He couldn't put his name down unless he was there, so we just left it blank. You have to do that, or else you could have women making up all sorts of stories. I could have put Tom Cruise down as your dad, couldn't I?' Being young, I'd accepted her word trustingly. But I'm holding Dani's certificate and his name is on there, and he wasn't present for that either – I remember sitting in the office with Mum and then going to McDonald's to celebrate my sister being made into an official person. The fact that she deliberately left Dad's name off the certificate tells me something. If she had wanted to hide her infidelity then she would have named him as my father. But he must have known from birth that I was another man's child. They only married six months before I was born, probably because she was pregnant. It's strange trying to imagine my father as a decent human being. At one point, however, he must have loved Mum enough to marry her, for him to try and raise me as his own. For a second, just a second, I can picture him with his arms around a sobbing Mum, telling her that it's okay, he'll look after her and the baby. What happened to turn him into the man who smashed me face-first into a coffee table and left me bleeding on the floor?

Perhaps if I searched through this squalor I would find

an answer of sorts. Maybe one day, when she's ready to open up again, Mum will be able to tell me. Right now, I need to forget him and focus on getting things sorted before the trial, making sure that Dani is stable and safe.

I fold our birth certificates up and put them in my purse. Dani emerges from upstairs, kicking two or three bags in front of her. She is carrying her school bag, but it seems to be weighed down by hair styling appliances.

'Have you got everything you need?' I ask. 'We won't be coming back here.' She nods and glances around, taking in a last view of her childhood home. I feel no such nostalgia for the building. She looks up at the ceiling.

'Could we give it a bit of a poke?' she asks. 'Might be fun to watch the bath fall through.'

'Get in the car.'

It takes three trips up and down the drive to load everything into my tiny Citroen. I run almost at a crouch, ducking behind my car as I stuff bin bags into the back seat. Even after all these years, I will do anything to avoid meeting Dad.

We're in the supermarket buying croissants when my phone rings. I take the call, a finger stuffed into my right ear to block out the screams of a sugar-hungry toddler in the biscuit aisle. Dani leans against the trolley, staring at me intently.

Because we're in a public place I restrict myself to saying, 'Thank you, thank you for letting me know.' I put my phone back in my pocket and run my fingers through my fringe.

'Oh, damn,' is all I can manage.

Dani leans over the trolley's handle.

'What?' she demands. 'It's Mum isn't it?'

'No, that was the court clerk. They're dropping the charges against me. The witnesses have withdrawn their statements.' I press my hands against my mouth. They are trembling rather violently.

Perhaps my advice to Tom appealed to his better nature. Perhaps he took the decision as we walked into court and he realised the impact his words would have on my life – after all, he ran like a rabbit first chance he got. It doesn't matter. All that matters is that he told the truth.

A smile of Grinch-like proportions spreads across Dani's face. Then she grabs my wrists and jumping up and down with excitement she screams, drawing the attention of every single shopper in the store. The relief hits me like a drug, and I find myself dancing down the bakery aisle with her.

The relief doesn't last long. We arrive home and I'm confronted by the bare cupboards and fridge, Dani's clothes still in bin bags and officious voicemail messages from the school and social services. I feel that familiar sense of dread creeping back into my bones. Yes, I've escaped a prison sentence, but the case against me being dropped is not the same as a unanimous not guilty verdict. There's no guarantee that St. Luke's will have me back and, without a job, how am I going to afford to feed and clothe the two of us, and keep a roof over our heads? Geoffrey will push hard to have me dismissed, and all I can do is hope that my guardian angel can once again come to my rescue. I take my phone out of my pocket, and dial her number.

15

The clock's fingers creep towards 2.30, and there are butterflies rattling around inside my stomach. They're going to be a proper handful, they always are last thing on a Friday. Especially this Friday.

I stand in the doorway and wait for them to line up neatly. They enter my space on my terms. I wait until everyone is lined up quietly against the wall before saying, 'Dewch i mewn.' Fifteen students enter the room and take their seats. Those who have brought bags take out their pencil cases. A very few take out battered writing books.

'Prynhawn da, dosbarth 11Y.'

'P'nawn da, Miss Bennett.'

'Last lesson before your exams,' I say. The day they have dreamed of since Year 7 is finally upon them. Friday, fifth period: their last lesson with me and their last lesson as Year 11 students.

The class has depleted somewhat in size since my return to St. Luke's. Alicia, understandably, has not forgiven me for telling her to shut up. Nia dropped out in protest. Four other parents requested that their children be removed from my care, preferring to believe the rumours that I was indeed guilty, but someone 'high up' had mysteriously intervened on my behalf and magically persuaded the CPS to drop all charges.

Surprisingly, Tom was not one of those who moved classes. His dad even came to parents' evening and offered me a tattooed hand to shake, by way of an apology.

'Fair dos to you, Miss Bennett. Not many teachers would have the lying little scrote back in class after what he's done. We appreciate it, we really do.'

Tom, late as usual, saunters into class. There is no need for me to mention the seating plan. He takes his seat at the front of the class blithely, blanking Cassie completely. She examines her manicured nails and feigns indifference.

The truth about Tom's injuries came out eventually, and to tell the truth, it is disappointingly prosaic. It was revealed that Cassie had been cheating on Tom (or cheating on the other guy, depending on whose version you hear). She'd succeeded in working the other guy into such a jealous rage that he and a gang of friends decided to 'teach the cocky little shit a lesson'. Details of the tit-for-tat brawls which followed are a little confused; suffice to say that Tom ended up with a fractured eye socket and a broken ulna. Tom admitted it was Cassie's idea to blame me for the assault, because of all of the bad blood between us.

Their plan backfired spectacularly when Tom was overcome by guilt. Cassie was dumped by both boys, who are now on cordial terms with one another, and she is universally known as 'Cassie Slag'. Her parents came and grovelled for my forgiveness in a most satisfactory manner, saying that she needed every GCSE grade possible to continue her academic career. I graciously forgave her, but only because I knew it would annoy her to continue sharing a classroom with Tom. Her destination for sixth form is an all-girls' private school in England. I can only hope that it is run by nuns.

Once the story became public knowledge the accusations against me became nothing more than a footnote. As Mrs Court says: today's news is tomorrow's chip paper. I was back teaching at St. Luke's within a week of the court date.

I walk around the class handing out brown C2 envelopes. The students imagine that they contain some kind of parting gift, and tear them open eagerly. Ha, ha, ha. No, I've prepared them a revision pack containing mock exam papers and a vocab sheet. There is a small gift in there though: a biro printed with

CYMRU and the *draig goch* as a reminder of their time in my Welsh class. If they bother to turn up for the exam, I at least hope that they will remember to bring the pen with them.

'We'll quickly go over your revision packs ...' I say, enjoying the spectacle of fifteen students visibly wilting in their seats. 'Or perhaps you'd prefer to read them at home and come to see me next week, if there's anything you're unsure of.' Who am I kidding, the papers will be used as spit wads and confetti before the last bell rings. I've done my best, but I'm no miracle worker. 'You need any help, you know where I am. *Hwyl fawr a phob lwc.* Go on, clear off, the lot of you.' I dismiss them early, in keeping with tradition. Last lesson they bring out the board markers and biros to write messages on one another's polo shirts; then they run riot in the central courtyard with flour and eggs and bottles of water. They are let out early and sent on their way, so that by 3.30 the chaos is largely over and the other students can go home unmolested.

I'm surprised, and rather touched, when they upend their chairs, placing them neatly on the tables, and then wait silently to be released. It seems like a last gesture of respect, an acknowledgment that we finally came onto the same page and started to function and to learn together.

I go to the door, and for the last time, I open it and dismiss 11Y. The last few weeks have been tolerable, but in truth, I am not sorry to see them go. Tom is one of the last to leave.

Many of my colleagues have expressed amazement that I didn't push for him to be excluded or punished. They can't understand how I can continue to teach him, when he came within an atom's width of destroying my career. Yet, even after all he has put me through, I find that I don't actually hate Tom. I don't like him and I never will, but I find myself able to tolerate his presence in my lessons. Perhaps it's because I see something of myself in him, or rather, of who I used to be. He's become different from the others, in a kind of old-head-young-shoulders way. He may have been a little shit, but he did the right thing in the end, and importantly, he did it of his own accord. For that at least, he deserves a second chance.

He swings his back pack up onto his shoulder, then pauses in the doorway and gives me the slightest of nods.

'Look after your mum, miss.' He has never apologised for his behaviour; but he never fails to ask after Mum's health. I return his nod, curtly. 'And stay out of prison, miss.'

Without missing a beat, I reply, 'You too, Tom.'

He's gone. He's someone else's problem now. I close the door and lean against it momentarily. This is a big day for me too. My first Year 11 class have flown the nest, and more importantly, despite Geoffrey's continued efforts to make things difficult, I survived them.

I go from desk to desk, picking up the remaining empty chairs and turning them upside down. Bev the cleaner always seems to make a bit more effort to keep my room looking presentable, and I like to think it's because I try to make it easier for her to do her job.

A knock on the door. It's Cathy Art, carrying two mugs of herbal tea. She smiles nervously, almost apologetically.

'Well, they're gone,' she says, offering me the Garfield and Nermal mug. I take it with a smile.

'Does the last day of term feel this good?' I ask.

'Not quite, because you know they're coming back next year.' That is an uncharacteristically sour thing for Cathy to say, but she hasn't been quite herself these past few weeks. Her usual bohemian chic, which usually gives her such an air of *je ne sais quoi* has deteriorated into *dragged backwards through a hedge*. In all honesty, she looks like someone who has trouble getting out of bed in the mornings.

'Cathy, I don't mean to be nosy, please tell me to keep my beak out if you want … but are you all right?' She shakes her head and I see tears filling her eyes. She looks so exhausted, so defeated. I've felt like that myself on many an occasion. I put down my mug and hug her. She leans against me for the briefest second, then steps back and dries a few tears with her sleeve.

'I'll be okay in a minute …' she croaks, composing herself. 'There's something I wanted to talk to you about. I've gone and done something …'

'You're not leaving?' I ask, anxiously. After Mrs Court, Cathy is my closest ally.

She goes to the window and looks down at the Year 11s running around the car park, spraying one another with silly string.

'You know I had that really bad lesson observation with the Head last month … since then he's had me on an improvement plan. Weekly meetings, random drop-ins … I can't do it any more, Cat. He's such a bastard. I hate him, I absolutely hate him.' She turns to me, her eyes sparkling with tears she can no longer repress. 'It's nothing to do with my teaching. I wouldn't mind if his criticism was constructive, but it isn't. It's personal. Last week he called me a lefty woolly liberal. I told him that was totally inappropriate, but he just smirked like he always does and said, "I've not written it down, have I?" It's bullying, Cat. I can't take any more, so I've decided I'm going to file a written complaint against him.'

'Good for you,' I say.

'And I've found out since that I'm not the only one. Vicky English is doing it too, because he accused her of acting in a sexually provocative manner towards her male students.' I snort with laughter at this, because Vicky is a puritanical old woman in a thirty-year-old body. She wears floor-length skirts and 80 denier tights, even in summer. She proudly boasts that she has never once plucked her eyebrows or coloured her hair. It is just her misfortune to have an absolutely huge pair of tits.

Seriously, her boobs enter the staff room a good ten seconds before she does.

Cathy continues, 'Steph Geography is raising a grievance. And Matty, that little student teacher who was with us in the Easter term, she's written a complaint. Geoffrey gave such a negative report to her university tutor that she's been told she may fail her PGCE. Apparently he told her to get out of the classroom and stop wasting everybody's time.'

'Just what you need to hear right at the very start of your career,' I add. He said something similar to me, just after I joined the Welsh department. I chose to ignore him and listen to Mrs Court's feedback instead.

'There are other people complaining, a few blokes included; but it seems as though he's really got something against female teachers. Listen, I know you didn't complain about his behaviour when you were suspended, but we all think you should have. He really mishandled things, he manhandled you and did his best to make life difficult for you. Why don't you make a complaint at the same time? He gets one or two every year, but somehow he gets them swept under the carpet. If you and me, Steph, Vicky and Matty all complain at the same time then maybe we will actually achieve something collectively.'

'What do you hope to achieve?' I ask cautiously. I would love nothing more than to see smug tosspot Geoffrey suffer, but he is made of Teflon and nothing ever sticks to him.

'We need to get him out of here. We need Fenella in post, as acting headmistress, before ESTYN comes here next year.'

'Does Mrs Court know about this?'

'I think she's aware of the rumblings of discontent. She knows that three female teachers have handed in their notice this term alone, and I've mentioned more than once that I'm considering leaving. We don't feel respected here. We don't feel safe. How are we supposed to do our jobs when we know that we'll be undermined and humiliated in front of our colleagues and students by the very person who is supposed to protect us from false allegations?' She pauses for breath, her cheeks pink with emotion.

I perch on the edge of my desk, thinking back to Vicky's warning in the staffroom. 'I thought the Head hated me because I was an ex-student. Could it be something more?'

'Consider this, Caitlin: the Welsh department is the only all-female department in the entire school. Even the home economics teacher is an ex-naval chef. He promotes men over women, every time. Look at how he handles accusations against men too – he believes their version of events unquestioningly. But in your case, everybody thought that he was giving you short shrift. Same with students – he only raises his voice to girls.'

'Probably because he knows that someone like Tom could punch his lights out.' I've thought about doing it many times since returning to St. Luke's, but I won't give him the satisfaction of sacking me for gross misconduct.

'Exactly,' says Cathy, relieved that we're on the same page. 'Well, I've had enough. We have to highlight his bullying and make him accountable.'

'Then let's do it,' I exclaim. 'It's time for Geoffrey the Teflon Tosser to come unstuck.'

'I've already made a start,' she says, with a sinister little smile. She beckons me to the window and points down at the car park. 'I know it was terribly wrong of me, but earlier today he told me that perhaps I should consider leaving at the same time as Year 11, jumping before I was pushed …'

'He never said that?'

'Oh, he did. He's already told me that he wants to cut down the curriculum time devoted to art, with a view to making redundancies next year. Forewarned is forearmed, he said. Anyway, he said that and waltzed off, leaving me bloody fuming. And I was holding a packet of Post-it notes at the time and ... well, I'm afraid I just flipped.'

'What did you do?' She points down to the car park, to a shining blue hatchback. Geoffrey's pride and joy. He has a parking space reserved for him, but refuses to park in it, preferring to hide its metallic lustre amongst our cheaper, older automobiles. The story goes that he arrives early and leaves late, not because he is punctilious, but so that students will not be able to identify (and vandalise) his precious car.

'See that?' Cathy points a chipped fingernail at the bonnet of the car.

'What?'

'The Post-it note.' I squint and can just about make out a little square of yellow paper. It now forms part of a striking picture: a giant cock and balls that has been spray-painted onto the roof of the headmaster's car.

16

At 3.45 I meet Danielle outside the main entrance. Normally I work late and she walks home with friends, but Fridays are different. I ask after her day, but I'm only half listening. My mind is already racing ahead to what I'll wear for my date.

Mum is out at her yoga class, and Dani goes straight to her room to change out of her uniform. She too is in a rush to get out and maximise the time she can spend down the park with her mates. When she was living with Mum and Dad she came and went as she pleased, and considered getting home before 11pm an 'early night'. As soon as she moved in with me I slapped a 9pm curfew on her. The first few weeks were a battle of wills, but I won every time with the argument, 'Don't like my rules? Go and live with Dad.' She can't even call my bluff, because there's been no contact from Dad for several months. The housing association has repossessed their old house. Any appeals to Mum are always met with the same reply of, 'Do what your sister says, Danielle. This is her house.'

On a weeknight we all eat together, but on Fridays and Saturdays Dani goes straight out to meet her friends. She'll grab a bag of chips for tea. I don't particularly like that she leaves Mum at home on her own, but I can't say anything, as that's exactly what I intend to do.

Mondays, Tuesdays, Wednesdays and Thursdays are for cooking, planning, cleaning and marking. Sundays, when Chris isn't at work, he'll travel down to see his daughters. But Friday and Saturday nights are set aside for us to spend together. It's lucky that neither of us has much in the way of an alternative social life.

I meet Chris at 233, a new bar on the High Street. He's sitting at the bar, a bunch of flowers resting next to his pint.

'Hello, gorgeous,' he says, kissing me. I return the kiss

demurely, although I'm already aching to bury my face in his neck, inhale his aftershave and nibble at his throat. Friday is 'date night', flowers and a meal out somewhere. Saturday night is our 'at home' time. His insistence on this ritual wooing is rather sweet, but after five days of nothing more than exchanging text messages, his every little touch, even the sight of the muscles bulging under his T-shirt, sends me into a frenzy. I would be happy if Friday night consisted of him handing me a bunch of flowers, then throwing me over his shoulder and giving me a fireman's lift up to his bedroom. He enjoys eating out, but I also think he enjoys toying with me and making me wait. Prick.

He's smiling now, his dark eyes staring into mine. He can read my thoughts.

'How was your day?' He's determined to drag this out, a nice, leisurely conversation before we move on to the restaurant for tea. (Or supper, as he calls it. He is distinctly more middle class than I will ever be.)

'Good. Year 11 left, they vandalised Geoffrey's car with a giant cock, and I've been drawn into a plot to help oust him.'

'Oust the cock?'

'You know what I mean. A mass complaint against him.'

'Have you checked with your union before doing this? Have you checked if you're actually in a union?' I lean over and flick his arm in playful annoyance.

'Anyway, Year 11 have gone. The countdown to the end of term has begun.'

'Ah yes, holidays. God forbid you teachers have to work for more than ten weeks in a row.'

'Keep going like this and you'll end up home alone, eating a ready meal for one.'

'No, I won't,' he murmurs, still smiling devilishly. Underneath the bar, his fingers are walking slowly up my knee towards the hem of my dress. 'Would you like a drink, or shall we move on to the restaurant?'

'We've got time for a quick one, haven't we?' I raise my hand and the bar tender comes over. 'House white, spritzer. With soda. Thanks.' While the bar tender's back is turned I lean across and deftly walk my hands up Chris' inner thigh, aiming for his crotch. He pushes me away, but already I can see a slight bulge in his jeans.

The bartender catches me in the act.

'Y'know, there's a hotel across the street if you two want to get a room. Just saying.'

'You should be used to us by now, Justin,' I say. A beeper sounds. That beeper is the worst thing, no, the second worst thing, about dating a firefighter. You can't complain if your night is ruined, because while you are finishing your meal alone and watching yet another reality TV show, your partner is out there risking his or her life to help others.

Chris glances down at his pager. 'It's a shout. Looks like you'll be eating the meal for one, not me.' He pulls on his jacket, then leans over and kisses me.

'Stay safe,' I tell him.

'Now, where's the fun in that?' he replies, walking towards the door. The absolute worst thing about dating a firefighter is not the disruption, it's not the restrictions because he's on call, or even seeing him come home stressed and tired. No, the worst thing about dating a firefighter is that little voice which whispers each time he walks out of the door, *What if this is the last time you see him alive?* You have to learn to silence the voice, dismiss the thought and resist the urge to run after him for one last hug and kiss. You tell yourself that yes, one day he may go to a major incident and not come back. But that's true of everybody, really – anybody could walk out of their front door and get hit by a bus. But when your boyfriend's job frequently involves walking into burning buildings, you can't help but be aware that the odds are stacked against him.

In spite of this, I'd never, never ask him to consider a less risky career for my sake. He loves the job, and like me, the hardships are justified by the knowledge that he's making a difference. Fear is something I'm learning to live with, once again – except that I'm no longer afraid for myself. I no longer dream about being buried alive. I like awake at night worrying that Dad will show up again and lure Dani away from us with the promise of freedom and booze. Every time I receive an incoming call from a withheld number I brace myself that it could be bad news, either about Chris, or about Mum. Mum is my main worry. Her medication is working, but not as quickly or effectively as we'd hoped. As well as the worry of something happening to Chris, I live every day with the possibility that one day she'll slip back through the net, and I won't be there to catch her.

For the first month or so after she came out of the unit, Dani and I made sure that she was never alone for more than a few hours at a time. We drew up a timetable of volunteer work, exercise classes and family time, and we made sure that she stuck to it rigidly. It sounds awful, to say that we chaperoned and micro-managed our own mother in this way; in fact there were days when she accused me of being a bigger bully and control freak than my father ever was. But Mum is rather like a child, and although she initially resisted, she actually thrives on routine. Getting her out of the house, away from her own dark thoughts and into the fresh air really seems to be helping. She's embraced yoga in a big way, and she goes for coffee with 'the girls' after each lesson. She enjoys volunteering in a charity shop, although she's always buying crap she doesn't need. Her possessions take up so much floor space that Dani has had to move into my bedroom. Recently she's even started applying for retail jobs. I'm hoping she gets one at a stationer's or a cake shop, so she'll start bringing something useful home, rather than another set of novelty champagne flutes or a broken Teasmade.

We are making progress, but occasionally there are days when we take a step backwards. I know that today will be one of those days before I've even set foot through my front door. It feels as though I've developed some kind of sixth sense, when in reality I've just become very good at reading the little signs: every light in the house is on, even the table and bedside lamps. The house is ablaze with light. As I put my key in the lock I spy the TV, its sound muted. Adverts especially seem to enrage her.

'It's me!' I call, cheerfully but keeping my voice low. She hates excessive noise. 'Chris went out on a call, so I thought I'd come home rather than wait for him.' No answer. I go through into my miniscule kitchen, where she has all the drawers open and is scrabbling through the cutlery tray, like a dog digging for a bone. She doesn't say anything or even acknowledge my presence.

I know what she's looking for. I go to the freezer and take out two ice packs. Without saying anything, I put a hand on her shoulder and wheel her away from the cutlery tray, guiding her towards the kitchen table. I place the ice packs into her hands and her fingers close about them like a Venus fly trap. She squeezes and squeezes until the pain becomes unbearable. She grits her teeth against the throbbing, burning cold. I watch her pain rise to the surface like a blister. As it bursts, so does she. Silent tears ooze down her cheeks. She cries for a few minutes, and once it is all over I take the ice packs from her and put them back in the freezer.

'Better?' I ask. She nods. I place a box of tissues in front of her. 'You should have called. I would have come straight away.'

'I didn't want to bother you,' she sniffs.

'You're never a bother,' I tell her, but I don't think she believes me.

'I hate feeling like this,' she says glumly. 'You'd think it would get easier, with time.'

'I think we need to go and see Dr Khan, check that you don't need your dosage upping. It doesn't seem to have been as effective these past few weeks.'

It's dangerous, using 'we'. Some days she'll say, 'I'm so lucky to have my girls.' Other days she'll tell me to piss off, that it's her body and she doesn't want me policing her, forcing her to take medication which is poisoning her and making her worse. Tonight however, she just smiles wanly.

I make her a cup of Moroccan tea, sweet with sugar. She catches my hand as I place the cup before her, and gives my fingers a gentle squeeze.

'Thank you, honey. I'm tired. I think I'll drink this in my room, go and do some breathing exercises.' She pads softly out of the kitchen, the hems of her palazzo pants brushing the floor. Yoga has given her a poise, a dancer's movement. She's ditched the oversized T-shirts and tracksuits in favour of tunics, loose trousers and headscarves, which she wears to cover her greying hair. The bleached blonde of her youth, she explained, was the last thing that 'belonged' to Dad. He liked blondes, and he liked her to be blonde. The hair had to go.

I wait until I hear her door closing, then I go to the hiding place and locate the key for the sharps cupboard. I retrieve a sharp knife, carve myself a few slices of cheese, then I wash the knife, dry it, replace it in the rack, padlock the cupboard shut and then conceal the key back in its hiding place. I should really just develop a taste for goat's cheese and save myself a lot of hassle.

As usual, I feel a rush of guilt because I chose to go out and leave Mum on her own. It takes a moment for me to remember Andrea's advice. She's helping me to rationalise these guilty feelings, to acknowledge that Mum is a grown woman who ultimately must make her own choices. I shouldn't feel guilty for wanting some kind of life outside the walls of my home. We occasionally need some time apart, some breathing space. God knows there is precious little actual space in this house.

When Mum is watching one of those awful exploitative poverty porn documentaries, when Dani has annexed both my room and my laptop to do her homework, I will find myself locked in the bathroom. I'll roll a towel and put it against the bottom of the door in order to block out Danielle's execrable taste in music. (Do you have any idea how sickening Justin Bieber is to a goth who raised herself on Slipknot?) I'll sit on the floor, propped up against the tub, and mark a set of school books. Sometimes I'll just sit and read TES articles on my phone. Sometimes I'll sext Chris and we'll act out whole fantasies via text message. That tiny white cube has become my happy place, my refuge from the constant white noise of chattering kids, crap TV and even crappier music.

Sometimes I find it galling that I pay the rent and all the bills, yet the only space I can claim ownership of is the ten square feet between the bath tub and toilet. Even in halls at university, at least I had a bedroom to call my own. But I bite my lip, because Mum would take a complaint as a hint to vacate, and she's not ready for that, not yet. The plan is that she and Danielle will eventually get a place of their own, once Mum is working and well enough to live independently.

She returns to the kitchen as I'm finishing my sandwich.

'I just thought I'd let you know, honey ... I went to see a solicitor today. I've asked him to begin divorce proceedings against your father, if he can find him, to serve the papers.'

'Well, that's progress,' I say, unable to hide my surprise.

'Isn't it just? I felt so proud of myself for walking in there and saying, "My marriage is over. I would like to make it official." When the solicitor asked on what grounds I was divorcing him I ended up explaining about your dad and his drinking, and I think that's what triggered me earlier … thinking about everything that has happened, how I should have walked away sooner … Anyway, I told him, "Get me out of this. I don't care what reason you have to give. I'm happy to testify that my eldest child is a bastard, if I have to."

This causes me to choke on my sandwich. She pats my back and I cough up a phlegmy ball of dough.

'The wheels are finally in motion. Just thought I'd let you know, sweetie,' she says serenely, as she floats back up the stairs.

Half ten on a Friday night, and no sign of my sister. This does not make me a happy bunny. I begin to suspect that she regularly ignores the Friday night curfew, because she knows that Mum will not punish her. Eventually, I manage to get her on the phone.

'Do you know what a *nemesis* is, Danielle?'

She clears her throat. 'It's a righteous infliction of retribution manifested by an appropriate agent. Personified, in this case, by you.' She's seen the film. Damn.

'Correct. I am giving you exactly ten minutes to get your arse through this front door, Danielle, or I am coming for you.'

'I'm down by the dock, how am I supposed to get back in ten minutes?'

'Walk. Quickly. I mean it. Are you walking, Danielle? Because if I have to come out there and bring you home I am cutting up your mobile phone contract. You'll be on £5 a month pay as you go, until you leave school.'

'No!'

'If you break curfew one more time I will visit retribution

137

on your skinny little backside by grounding you for the summer holidays.'

'No! Oh God, I'm sorry, Cat!'

'Get your arse back here, now.'

'I'll be home in ten minutes.'

'You now have nine.'

She must have sprinted, because she arrives home with a couple of minutes to spare, contrite and apologetic. Too contrite. I lean in close and inhale. Her cheap body spray doesn't mask the scent of tobacco, mixed with something muskier, more pungent. She's been smoking weed possibly, and most likely drinking, in the company of someone who wears far too much aftershave.

'Who is he, Dani?' I demand.

'You told me to come home, and I came home. Don't start having a go at me.' She tries to barge past me, but I sidestep and catch her arm.

'You broke curfew and you've been with a man. Don't bother lying to me, I know every excuse in the book. Who is he? How old is he?' She pushes me away and races up the stairs. 'Dani!' I yell, exasperated. 'Don't come crying to me when you get knocked up and he doesn't want anything to do with you!'

At the top of the stairs she turns and practically screams at me, 'It's not like that! And you have no right to stop me from seeing him, you fucking control freak!' Then she goes into my bedroom and slams the door so hard that the whole house seems to shake.

'Danielle!' calls Mum, alarmed by the noise. I stand there for a second, staring up at my bedroom door and seething. 'You can't just go in all heavy-handed,' says Mum gently. 'Maybe in class, but at home …' I turn to look at her. It's on the tip of my tongue to snarl, What the hell do you know about raising teenagers? By the time I was Dani's age you'd handed me over to Social Services! I manage not to say it, because I don't want to bring about another relapse. However, she must see the rage in my eyes, because she suddenly averts her gaze and mutters, 'You do what you think is best. You're looking out for her, I know that.' Mum slinks back into the kitchen and unmutes the television. The whole house seems to pulse with Dani's music. I suspect she's found the cheesiest K-pop song on YouTube and cranked the volume up just to annoy me. As penance for mishandling the situation, I go and sit in the bathroom, with a rolled-up towel against the bottom of the door.

17

I put a red cross through the last box on my calendar and step back to admire it. The last day of the school year. Outside, in the corridor, the excitement is palpable. The whole building seems to crackle with a sort of electricity. Just one more day to get through. One day should be a breeze, given the year that I've had.

Somebody taps on the glass of my classroom door. It's an adult tap, an urgent yet polite one. I turn around to see Mrs Court being jostled by my Year 7 registration class, and hasten to let her in.

'7J, what are you doing?' I cry, putting on my best theatrically angry voice. 'Move out of the way for a senior member of staff! Line up against the wall and wait until the bell goes, or better still, go and burn off some energy on the playing field for ten minutes.' I wait until they either depart or form an orderly line against the left-hand wall, then I step back to admit Mrs Court into my room. 'If you're going to loiter, please do it quietly,' I tell them.

'Miss, what does loiter mean?'

'It's exactly what you're doing now, Theo.' I close the door gently and lock it after us.

'How can I help you, Mrs Court?' I ask. She walks over to the far corner of the room, out of sight of the door and, importantly, out of the students' hearing.

'I haven't got time to explain,' she whispers. 'I've just had some news. Good news. But before I can make it public I need to ask you a question. Caitlin, are you willing to be acting head of the Welsh department?' I gasp.

'Is Geoffrey ...?' I hardly dare voice the word. She nods, her smile growing bigger still. She uses her index finger to slash her throat.

'Ten staff members have put in written complaints against him, excluding yourself. The governors met yesterday, and he's been put on gardening leave, effective immediately. They've asked me to step in and be acting head, but I need to know that I can leave my department in capable hands. I know you've only been here a year, but I have every faith that you'll cope admirably ...'

'Yes!' I say, breathlessly. 'Of course!'

'It's happening, Caitlin. It's happening!'

Just then we hear Trevor Oare demanding of my students, 'Who said you could loiter here?'

'Miss Bennett,' they chorus. Mrs Court almost prances to the door, but as she steps out into the corridor she slows down and becomes almost regal in her bearing. I smile to myself. She looks every part the benevolent headmistress.

'*Dewch i mewn*, 7J!' I call brightly. 'Last day of the school year, last assembly, let's not be late!'

'Have you bought us any sweets, miss?' asks Callum impishly.

'Sorry, Callum, I haven't. But I'll bring you some back from my holiday, I promise.'

'Everyone, miss, or just me?'

'Everyone, of course.'

'Where are you going, miss?'

'The Seychelles.'

'Where's that?'

'A long way from here.' Far enough that there's no chance of me running into any of my students.

'Who you going with? What are sweets like in the Seychelles?' I ignore the first question.

'I don't know what sweets are like in the Seychelles. I guess we'll find out when I bring some back, won't we?' Never let students into your private life, never let them get too close. The one and only time I broke that rule was when I met Tom

141

outside the magistrates' court. I appreciate that when I let my guard down, I got lucky. Where he saw vulnerability, others might have seen weakness. He withdrew his complaint against me; others might have scented blood and taken advantage of my emotional, shocked state. However, the mask is firmly back in place and I'm determined not to let it slip again.

A message is circulated, announcing an impromptu lunchtime staff meeting. I'm supposed to be watching over the student toilets and cloakroom, but the secretary tells me that 'Fenella specifically asked for you to be there.'

I get there at 12.35, straight after the lunch bell has sounded. The staff room is already packed. Everybody wants to find out if the rumours regarding Geoffrey's sudden departure are true.

I squeeze against the back wall, sandwiched between a radiator and filing cabinet. Cathy passes me a mug of tea; peppermint and liquorice in a Captain Planet mug that has probably been here since the 80s.

Mrs Court enters the room to address the troops.

'You may have heard rumours regarding the Headmaster. The facts of the matter are this: he has been the subject of a number of complaints, some of which, if proven, may be classed as gross misconduct. It is highly likely that his gardening leave will stretch into the autumn term. For the duration of the investigation I will be acting head. I've called you here today because I know you are all tired and morale is low. I wish the new term to be a new beginning for us all, which is why I thought it prudent to gather you here today and begin a dialogue regarding the future of St. Luke's.'

Some of the teachers have been here as long as my novelty cartoon mug, and probably won't take kindly to the sweeping new changes she is about to introduce. Any leader who comes in hoping to implement 'radical' changes is usually regarded as a bit of a snake oil salesman. Mrs Court has the virtue of being the school's longest-serving staff member, and one who has worked her way up through the ranks. However, she is also regarded as a bit of a maverick and a risk taker. Case in point: she was the only member of senior management who refused to expel me or transfer me to another secondary school, even after I incited a protest (riot) over Geoffrey's plans to introduce a mandatory skirt-only uniform for female students. She will have a difficult time convincing some of the more exhausted and cynical staff that her new policies will be worth the trouble of implementing. She begins her speech by acknowledging this.

'I am very aware of the magnitude of the task I have taken on. Let us be completely honest, within the confines of this room: St. Luke's is failing. Despite our best efforts as individual teachers, we are failing. Our results, our staff turnover, our sickness and attendance rates speak for themselves. Something needs to change. It may not be a surprise to you that the Headmaster and I did not always see eye to eye. His strategies and mine are very different. I am quite willing to admit that I fully intend to use the time given to me, however long or short it may be, to overhaul this school's procedures and systems.' She glances down at her notes for the briefest second, then raises her eyes to meet those of her colleagues.

'Let me share with you a story. Put your feet up, help yourself to a drink, I'm afraid it's going to be a long one ...' A few half-hearted chuckles from one corner of the room. 'Around a decade ago I met a young woman, a student here. She had boundless energy, but it was not being channelled into anything productive.' I have a horrible, sneaking suspicion that I am the young woman in the story, but she doesn't betray me by looking in my direction. 'I knew she required more support from us, but she was one of hundreds of students I taught, and although I sensed that something was terribly

143

amiss in her home life, I failed to investigate thoroughly or to act in her best interests.' At this point one or two of the longest-serving staff members glance in my direction. I feel my cheeks flush hot with embarrassment. I fix my eyes on Mrs Court and ignore those looking at me. 'It wouldn't be right of me to go into details of her private life, but I can tell you that she ended up being hurt very badly. I went to the hospital with her; but the next day I was needed back in the classroom. I know some of my more senior colleagues may be angry with me for saying this, but as a staff, we utterly failed in our duty towards her. The Headmaster, her form tutor, her head of year ... we all asked questions of her, but none of us really *listened* to her answers. I criticise the senior staff, as Geoffrey's departure means that I am the only serving SMT member who knew her, and I have judged myself harshly over the years for not intervening sooner. I might have saved her a great deal of suffering. However, after she recovered she came back to sit her remaining exams, and stayed on for the sixth form. With a little extra support, her progress was remarkable. In less than a year I saw one of our worst behaved students become one of our brightest stars, and she is still shining brightly today.' She takes a deep breath, and finally she looks over at me. 'This young woman's suffering opened my eyes to what is wrong with how this school operates. Through her eyes, I saw how our education system is failing our young people, simply by not sufficiently taking their personal, pastoral and developmental needs into account. She also opened my eyes to what is possible if someone is properly guided and supported. Her progress was simply phenomenal. I believe that each and every child has incredible potential, if only we can work out how to best tap into it.' I swallow hard and sip my tea. 'I strive to replicate her success with each and every individual sent to my door, and I like to think that these individual interventions are successful. But for us to really tackle problems we need an overhaul. I know not all of my ideas will be popular, and some may not work out as intended, but we must try, and we must be open to change. We must be willing to learn from our mistakes. I will be speaking to each of you individually over the coming weeks about what we can and must do to improve St. Luke's. We have to raise standards, yes, but we all must look to improve our pastoral care, and how we support one another as educators. If you need something for your department, if you have ideas, problems or concerns, my door is always open. All I can promise is that I will give you my very best, and I will listen to everything you have to say. I hope that we will move forward together. Are there any questions?'

No questions, but a smattering of applause begins in the English department's corner and quickly spreads around the room. She clasps her hands against her skirt and smiles at her staff. The applause grows louder. Even though it is the end of term and we are all tired, we muster to her rallying cry. Even the older staff members, who've served under more education secretaries than I've had birthdays, look quietly optimistic.

'Enjoy your holidays, everybody. I look forward to a new start in September,' says Mrs Court. Cathy turns to me.

'Wow, she's really determined to grab this place by the scruff and give it a good shake, isn't she? She won't be teaching any more, I take it? Presumably that means there's a vacancy for a certain bright star looking to head her own department ...'

'I'm acting head of Welsh,' I whisper. She gives me a delighted little punch on the arm. A few others smile at me, having guessed that I am the girl in the story. To my horror, I see Baldy Pearson making his way over to me. I turn to flee, but in doing so I knock my mug of tea all over the table. I grab a handful of scrap paper from the waste-paper box and try to mop up the brown liquid. He stops directly in front of me, but before he can open his mouth I blurt out, loudly, in front of everyone, 'Mr Pearson ...' He holds up an index finger to silence me.

'I said at the start of term, Caitlin, call me Evan not Mr Pearson. You're a colleague now, not a student. I wanted to congratulate you on your appointment as head of the Welsh department. The youngest in the school's history, I believe.'

'Oh, I'm just the acting head because there's no one else in the department to do the job ...'

'Well, should you apply for the job proper, I am sure you have a good chance of getting it ... Provided you keep your temper!' He winks, to show that he is joking – but the point is a valid one, and well made. 'Mrs Court has been a good mentor.'

I force a smile and duck out of the staffroom, uneasy at being singled out so publicly. I head back to the Welsh department. Three classrooms, their doors glowing red beneath the large CROESO sign. One day soon, all this will be mine: the best equipped classroom, the biggest store room, an office of my own and a computer that actually works properly.

I see Mrs Court walking down the other end of the corridor, the hem of her long skirt swishing from side to side.

'Caitlin, there you are!' she calls. She beckons me over to her office. 'Now, I don't want you spending all your holidays here. Come in for a few days before the end of the holidays and we'll allocate sets and finalise the schemes of work. But you don't really have anything to worry about until the new term.' She unlocks the door and I follow her inside. 'I didn't embarrass you too much in there, did I?'

'Just a little,' I admit. 'I'll get over it.'

She leans against her desk and folds her arms against her chest, a pose I realise that I've been unconsciously imitating since I became Miss Bennett. Her brows narrow in a frown.

'I did ask myself whether it was wise to share such a personal story with the staff. I had my misgivings, but on the whole, as long as you aren't too angry with me, I'm glad that I did. I thought it was important for them to realise that my desire to bring about change comes from a need to help others, rather than a desire to further my reputation.'

'I don't think anybody would ever accuse you of that,' I tell her.

She bends, picks up an empty cardboard box and places it on the desk. As she loads the contents of her drawers into the box she talks animatedly about her plans for the new school year. I think of her masterplan folder, how many hours she must have spent researching and developing it. Finally, after years of waiting, she has the opportunity to put it into practice. I know that she will spend every day of her six weeks off planning and preparing for the new term.

18

Alone in my new office, I take possession of my kingdom. I begin by dragging the desk to a position against the back wall, so that I can see out of the window. My view is of the school's quadrangle, with its terracotta plant pots and memorial benches to pupils who died in the last century. I sit in the padded computer chair, enjoying the novelty of being able to swivel and twist the seat.

I like it here. It may only be a shoebox-sized office with a few filing cabinets, but already it is beginning to feel like a home of sorts. The green-grey carpet, the same carpet that was laid in the classrooms when I was a student here, seems to be ingrained with a fine white dust. Instead of the odour of sweat and unwashed uniforms, this room smells faintly and pleasantly of chalk. Old black and white school photos hang on the wall, presumably from the beginning of Mrs Court's career. They give the room an air of timelessness, of belonging to the age of cap and gowns and canes. This room is a little time capsule.

But the photos are not mine. I remove them carefully from the wall to transfer them to Mrs Court's new office. The last frame, almost concealed by a filing cabinet, does not contain a photo at all; rather it is a printed copy of a poem. I glance at the title, but do not need to read the poem. I know it already, by heart.

In the summer before I went to university to begin my teaching degree I met with Mrs Court several times. She had just been promoted to deputy, and had lost her husband to cancer two terms previously. I'd just completed my first anger management course, and was getting ready to move out of children's home and into the university halls of residence. Over the course of that summer holidays we met for coffee four or five times. They were slightly awkward meetings, partially because of the lingering teacher-pupil dynamic, but also because I was adjusting to my newfound status as an adult and she was adjusting to life as a widow. She was grieving, and I didn't know what to say to comfort her. Our conversations mainly revolved around my plans for the next four years. She'd arrive at each coffee shop or café with a small gift: a book she'd found useful, or the phone number of a teacher who might be able to offer me a work placement. I was the recipient of her years of experience, and after each meeting I wrote much of her advice in a little pink notebook. I still have that notebook.

One August afternoon we met for the last time. As we rose to our feet and bid one another goodbye, I surprised myself by hugging her. She reached into her voluminous teacher's holdall and produced a parcel, rectangular and thin, wrapped in brown paper. She told me to open it after she'd gone, and to be careful as it was fragile.

From the shape and feel of the parcel I knew it contained a photo frame, but I was curious as to what image she could have found worthy of making into a gift. My time at school had been miserable and my classmates had disliked me. Anything school-related would seem inappropriate. Curious and impatient, I opened it on the bus ride back to the home. Beneath the paper, covering the glass, was another sheet of paper on which she'd written this message: *I found this helpful. May it also inspire and drive you. Never lose sight of who you are, Caitlin. With very best wishes, Fenella Court.*

I raised the paper to discover a poem, 'Invictus'. Everybody who has read 'Invictus' remembers its last two lines. For me, it is the last couplet of the second stanza.

I run my finger along the top of Mrs Court's framed copy, cleaning off the thick grey layer of dust which has gathered over the years. Just as I am about to ring her and ask whether she wants her frames bringing down, there is a knock on the door. I turn around to see Geoffrey standing there, looking at me. At least he has the decency to wait for me to open the door, rather than entering unasked.

'I thought you were on gardening leave,' I say, coolly. *Gardening leave, effective immediately* usually means you are escorted off the premises. He shouldn't still be sniffing around here.

He replies, with equal coolness, 'I'm looking for Fenella and I thought she might be here.'

'Last time I saw her she was down in the headteacher's office.'

'Can't wait to get her feet under the table.' He smiles a mirthless smile, probably intended to be wry. 'I'll go and find her, then I'll be off.' He turns to go, but as I move to close the door, he pauses and looks back at me. 'This is all a misunderstanding, Miss Bennett. Unlike yourself, I have made sure of my legal representation ...' The sneer in his voice is unmistakeable. 'Once they have cleared up these misunderstandings ...'

'All eleven of them,' I add, unable to help myself.

'... cleared up these *misunderstandings* ... Once I am back in my role as headmaster, I shall remember the names of those who supported me, and those who chose not to do so.' He turns and walks towards one of the fire exits, glancing out of the window and whistling tunelessly as he goes. For my sake, for everybody's sake, he *has* to get the sack.

However I don't have time to dwell on Geoffrey's veiled threat or even to celebrate surviving my first year in teaching or my temporary promotion. Once the school day is over it becomes a race to get things ready before Chris picks me up on the way to the airport. I told him that it was ambitious to catch a flight on the same day as the end of term, but agreed to it as the flights were a fair bit cheaper. I'm regretting it now, as I rush around double and triple-checking that everything is in place. The fridge and freezer are full, there's a food delivery ordered for next Friday and Mum's anti-depressant prescription is on repeat order, for her to collect next Wednesday. I've transferred an extra few hundred pounds into her bank account. Her signing-on appointment with the job centre, Dani's hockey club meetings and matches are written on the calendar, which I've left propped up against the kettle. I've hidden the key to the sharps' drawer by tucking it away inside a copy of the collected works of Marcus Aurelius.

I stand and survey the kitchen, wondering whether there's anything I've left undone.

I call up the stairs, 'Mum, Dani, I'm off soon!'

'Oh, are you going, darling?' Mum comes trotting downstairs, the sleeves of her silk kimono fluttering like wings of a butterfly.

'Where's Dani?'

'Out with her friends, I suppose.'

'Keep an eye on her, Mum. I know it's the holidays, but don't just let her come and go as she pleases. If she says she's stopping over with a friend, make sure you meet the parents, so you know she's not sneaking off to a nightclub or stopping over at a boy's house ...'

Once or twice in the past month Danielle casually mentioned that she was going for a 'sleepover' at a mate's house, but changed her mind as soon as I offered to drive her over. I'm a poacher-turned-gamekeeper, I can smell trouble a mile off. I shudder to remember what I did at her age. I'm lucky I didn't end up in a shallow grave, clutching a bottle of Aftershock and a quarter of skunk.

Mum is smiling, but the look in her eyes betrays her.

'What's wrong?' I ask.

'Nothing, darling.'

'Mum, if you don't tell me, I'll worry the whole time I'm away.'

'I don't want to be a bother … But your dad has been in touch.' We still call him Dad out of habit. There are a few other epithets I could give him, and as Mum hands me her mobile phone I curse under my breath, adding a few more choice names to the list. I scroll quickly over the text, feeling the blood draining from my face.

'Why didn't you change your number?' I demand.

'I forgot,' she says.

'Block him,' I order. 'You don't have to deal with his shit. Block him and ignore.'

'But what if he does what he says?' she asks.

> *Just to let you no I am going to go to court over custody of danielle. Whn you finalley top yrself I don't want hr left with that sycho bitch. No court will leave her with sum1 who keeps tryin to kill herself or a sister who is only half related and has been arested for assault.*

A bitterly ironic comment coming from someone who served a four-month sentence for assaulting me. You hideous man, why did you have to come crawling out of the woodwork? I scroll down to the next message, trying to keep my face relaxed even though my blood is rising to boiling point.

> *She is not safe with yu, an I am goin to get full custody and she cn come and live with me. Why dnt you just hurry up and do it? Dni is sick to death of you and Catlyn too I dnt doubt. Nbdy cares whether u live or die. Nbdy will miss u, so do us all a favour.*

'What do we do?' asks Mum, helplessly. I turn and look her in the eye.

152

'For a start, you ignore *everything* he says. You're beating the depression, you're moving on from him and getting your shit together. He's drinking again and he's doing this to try and push your buttons, to control you ...' Mum nods earnestly, biting her lip. 'I mean, everything he's written is complete bullshit. He must be off his face. There's no way he's going to take Dani away from us. If he tries anything, I'll sort it out. I'll stop him. As soon as I get back from holiday we'll sort this out, okay?' Mum nods again, trustingly. I hear a car horn beep, and realise that Chris is parked at the kerb, waiting for me. Damn it, if only I had an hour or so extra, so I wasn't leaving her in the lurch ... This news couldn't have come at a worse time. 'Screenshot the messages, Mum, and then block his number. Promise me that you won't respond to him. He wants to get you upset. Don't play his game.'

'I won't,' she replies. 'I wasn't sure whether to tell you, Caitlin, but I'm glad I did. You always know what to say to make it better. Thank you, sweetheart. You go on holiday and enjoy yourself. I promise you don't need to worry about me.' Chris is at the front door, and I can tell that he's impatient just by the way he knocks.

'You and Dani look after one another, okay? Keep an eye on her, Mum.' I open the door unwillingly, hating the fact that I'm leaving her just when she needs reassurance. Chris greets Mum with a smile, but he is squirming slightly. We're behind schedule, and he hates to be late – especially when faced with the vagaries of motorway traffic. 'I'm coming, I'm coming!' I tell him, and he takes the brand new suitcase from my hand.

'I'm sorry to be in such a rush, but there's heavy traffic on the A55,' he says apologetically to Mum.

'Off you go then!' she replies cheerfully, and stands at the door waving us off. I hope her relief is unfeigned, because although I'm blowing kisses and waving like a happy toddler, inside I'm still bloody fuming. The old fury is back in my blood. I want to punch Dad in the face, over and over and over, until he bleeds. If his goading triggers another suicide attempt from Mum, I swear to God that he will bleed. How dare he, how fucking dare he ignore his daughter for months on end, leave his wife in a psychiatric unit, and then suddenly waltz back into our lives and try to destroy the stability we've worked so hard to achieve?

'Anything wrong?' Chris asks.

'No,' I reply tersely. He glances down at my right hand, which is clutching the seatbelt across my chest.

'You shouldn't hold your seatbelt like that. Could stop it working properly in a collision.' I move my hand down to my lap. 'Now, tell me what's wrong.' He knows me too well to believe any further denial. As succinctly as possible, I tell him about Geoffrey's veiled and Dad's drunken threats: 'I know Dad's message may just be drunken shit-stirring, but what if he's serious? I mean, I very much doubt he'd get sole custody, but he could push for access, couldn't he? Mum hasn't got the money for solicitors, so I'd have to pay for that. Plus, it won't do Mum's mental health any good to have him raking up her suicide attempts and her bad parenting ... What am I supposed to do?'

'Nothing,' Chris soothes. 'I've been through all of this before with Melissa, and trust me – the best thing you can do now is absolutely nothing. Wait for your father to make the first move. Don't go and see a solicitor unless you get a letter from his, and that won't happen ... He's an unemployed alcoholic who went to jail for assaulting his child. No court in the land is going to award him sole custody, and it's unlikely he'll get unsupervised access either.' Chris's words have an instant calming effect. I realise that I have done exactly the same thing as I warned Mum not to do. I've allowed Dad to push my buttons, allowed myself to become disproportionately angry and blind to the facts. Chris continues, 'As for Geoffrey – write everything down and submit a report to the governors once you get back off holiday. He'll deny it of course, but it sounds as though he's for the chop, whatever he does. So put your feet up and forget about it all until we get back from holiday. What will you achieve by worrying constantly? Nothing, except spoiling your holiday. Don't give either of those arseholes the satisfaction.'

He's right – I shouldn't let Dad and Geoffrey cast a shadow over our first holiday as a couple. However, I also know it's not as simple as 'forgetting about it'. If it were, then Mum wouldn't have spent half her life fighting a battle to justify her own existence to herself. You can choose not to think about something, but even so, that 'something' creeps back into the quiet, empty moments, into sleep, into your gut and your intuition. I'd give anything to have a temporary kill switch for this temperamental mass of memories, synapses and chemical imbalances.

Chris reaches out and gently touches my thigh. 'You've got that thousand yard stare thing going on again. Come back to earth,' he says, taking his eyes off the road ahead just long enough to meet mine, to make me smile. He nods his head towards the glove compartment. 'Mind plugging the sat nav in, just so we can get an ETA?'

I open the glove compartment, but there's no sat nav inside. Instead, a white envelope drops out into the foot well. As I bend down to retrieve it I see CAITLIN written in Chris' near-illegible scrawl.

'What's this?' I ask.

'Open it,' he replies, smiling enigmatically. In my hands I am holding two airline tickets. First class. I'm speechless. They probably cost more than my car. 'I know it's your first time abroad and I want it to be special. And don't you dare offer to split the cost. It's my gift.'

'But why?'

'You've had a rough few months. I know a bit more leg room and some free champagne doesn't undo all the crap you've had to put up with, but I thought it might get the holiday off to a good start.'

'That it will, undoubtedly.' At the beginning of the relationship I felt awkward about Chris' insistence that he pay for the both of us. The words 'sugar daddy' kept creeping into my mind. Now I look at him and it dawns on me that I've been unchivalrous in doubting his motives. Chris' main concern in life is that the people around him are happy. Nobody has ever concerned themselves purely with my happiness. My safety, my mental and physical health, my career, my ambition, my guilt, my innocence, my anger – yes; but my happiness has never felt like much of a priority to anyone. I include myself in this neglect.

'Thank you,' I reply, suddenly choked with emotion. 'You are the kindest man I have ever met.'

'You deserve it,' he replies, and with that my kill switch is engaged. Dad, Geoffrey, Mum and Dani are left behind.

19

I wake up to the soft breaking of the waves outside our bedroom window. Every morning this week I've awoken and wondered whether I've been transplanted into someone else's life. This week has been a topaz in a sea of pebbles, or more prosaically, a flute of champagne in a fridge full of Special Brew. I'm not used to being this happy. If it wasn't for Chris at my side, snoring under the crisp white sheets, I'd worry that it was all a dream.

I roll onto my side and watch him sleeping. He is thirteen stone of perfection, apart from the tacky barbed wire tattoo snaking around his right bicep. Tattoo aside, I love everything about him. It's taken me a long time to admit that. For months and months I was scared to say it, even to myself, in case things went wrong. I wasn't going to get tied down by a man, oh no! Mum warned me not to commit myself; Dani told me I'd be choosing his nursing home. (She's fifteen. To her, a decade's age difference is almost a lifetime.) I laughed, agreed and told them that I was just using him for sex.

But last night, the last night of our holiday, the wall I'd built finally came tumbling down. He finally breached my defences, and no, that's not a sexual metaphor.

We were in a restaurant, having just finished our meal. I was sipping on some disgusting nightcap I'd ordered in an attempt to feel sophisticated. He saw that I was hating it, and offered me his port. Anyone can drink port, it's like a pudding. When I was a baby Nana used to put it on my dummy to suck.

As we were sipping our drinks Chris said, 'Listen, I've been thinking … now that your mum is talking about getting a place on her own … I think we need to move on from just seeing one another at weekends.' I looked down at my newly manicured nails. I was glad that he'd waited until the very last day of the holiday to have this conversation. This was the conversation I'd been dreading: Our Future as a Couple.

'Chris, if I was to consider moving in with someone I'd want there to be an understanding that it wasn't done in expectation of starting a family. You know I don't want kids.'

'Neither do I. Been there, done the 3am feeds and changed the nappies. Twice was enough for me.'

'Also, if we have the girls and Dani staying with us occasionally, we'll be needing a bigger place. We'd have to rent or buy together, but I'd want a written agreement: all costs split fifty-fifty, both jointly liable.' I've seen what happens when one partner controls the finances. He nodded in agreement, but I was just getting warmed up: 'I'd want to retain separate bank accounts, because I need to support Mum. And Dani is the named beneficiary on my life insurance and for my pension in-death benefits. I wouldn't change that until she's at least twenty-one, until she's old enough to provide for herself.' He was still nodding, albeit with less enthusiasm than before.

'I assume the conditions would also apply in the event of a more legally binding union?' He reached into his back pocket to produce a little black leather box.

'What's this?' I asked dumbly.

'It's a gift for the most kind and beautiful women I know …' I looked down at the ring, but it was unexpectedly blurred by tears. Nobody had ever called me kind or beautiful before – at least not when they were sober. 'The first time I met you, I knew that you had to be in my life. I can't explain why, but I trusted you instantly. Your honesty, determination, bravery … the way you always put other people before yourself … I've never known anyone like you.'

'Stop it,' I told him, as I turned into a flushed and tearful mess.

'I'm not going to stop. I want you to realise how wonderful you are. How happy you make me. I know we've not been together that long, but I love you, and I want to spend the rest of my life with you. Say you'll marry me.'

I looked into his eyes and saw that he was interpreting my contemplative silence and my tears as indecision. There was no indecision, none at all. I loved him for the same reasons. Without looking, I'd found my other half.

Chris opens his eyes, smiles sleepily and I get that little prickle of electricity running right through me.

'Good morning, Mrs Marston-to-be,' he says, reaching out and running his fingers along my jaw line. I shiver. His thumb brushes my lips tenderly. I kiss it. 'What time is it?'

'Time to get up, I'm afraid. We have to check out in three hours.'

He leans over and kisses me, slides his mouth over my throat. My arms go about his neck. 'We've got time, haven't we?' he asks. I break free from the embrace and roll out of bed.

'We can have sex at home. I'm going for a last swim in the sea.'

I open our veranda doors and step out onto sand so white it glistens like snow. Warm snow, shifting between my toes. He joins me, slides his arms around my waist and resumes kissing my neck.

Just before my heart stops beating, when I close my eyes for the last time, I know that I will remember this moment. It's right up there with trying on my cap and gown before the degree ceremony, or the moment Mrs Court offered me my job. I have a realisation that this is a moment to be absolutely savoured, because things cannot stay this perfect.

20

After a fourteen-hour flight I arrive home to find my front door wide open. Chris and I drag our suitcases into the lounge to find my sofa and dining chairs occupied by a gaggle of middle-aged women, with Mum at their centre. She is drinking prosecco through a straw, straight from the bottle, and cackling like a witch. These are not her lithe, genteel, quinoa-eating yoga friends.

'Mum!' I exclaim, dropping my bags.

'Caitlin!' She staggers to her feet and presses a pair of moist, plum-coloured lips to my cheek. She doesn't even smoke, yet I look down and see a fag smouldering in her hand. Several of her friends are sitting there, puffing away like chimneys. They are using my crystal pot-pourri bowl as an ash tray. It was my house-warming present from Mrs Court.

'Mum, you know I don't allow smoking in my house.'

'Nice way to greet your mother!' she exclaims, and turns away from me to pull a face at her new friends.

'Are you going to introduce me?'

'This is Caitlin, my eldest. Everybody, this is Caitlin. Caitlin, this is everybody. Let me get you a little drink, sweetheart ...' The uncertainty in her eyes as she glances from face to face tells me that she's out of her depth. She doesn't even remember the names of her visitors. It looks as though a whole pack of drunken women followed her out of the pub, lured by the promise of free booze from my cupboard.

'Did somebody order a stripper?' croaks one crone, squinting up at Chris through her electric blue eyeliner. They cackle with laughter, as one leans over the arm of the sofa and takes a swipe at his crotch.

'Did you bring a nice package for us?' More laughter. Chris shrinks back from their groping hands.

'What's going on, Mum?' I ask.

'This? Oh, this is just a little party we've been having, to celebrate my divorce. Why don't you join us? It's down to you, after all.' Little party, my arse. Stepping over empty bottles and discarded shoes, I go through into the kitchen. What has she been doing? I've been gone for two weeks. How is it possible that she could turn the house into such a shit tip in just two weeks?

There's a layer of grease on the hob, the bin is overflowing, and carrier bags full of takeaway cartons are piled high alongside it. The floor is sticky, there are hand prints on the unit doors, crumbs, and blobs of sauce, hairs, dirty pots and utensils on every surface. A pile of clothes has been dumped next to the washing machine, damp, and waiting to be hung out to dry. There are plastic bowls of dried cat food by the back door. I turn my head slightly and find a cat – a big black, malevolent tom cat – sitting at my feet, looking up at me.

'Why is this cat here?' I demand, a note of hysteria creeping into my voice. 'Whose cat is this?'

Chris comes over and rests his hand on my shoulder. 'Why don't you come back to mine, wait for the party to end and for your mum to clear up? I'm sure the cat will be gone by the time we come back.'

'Okay. I'll just use the loo and grab my keys and …' I break away from him. I don't really need the toilet, I just have to see the rest of the house. Ten seconds on the top landing is enough to start me hyperventilating. Mum's bedroom is so cluttered that there is only a doormat's width of floor space. You can't actually open her door properly because of the huge pile of clothes squashed behind it. Dani has left yellow liquid foundation all over my brand new bedding. My wardrobe has been ransacked, and half of my going out clothes have been discarded, tossed onto the floor. The bathroom has me gagging: brown stains in the toilet bowl, pubes stuck to the floor, more make-up on my fluffy towels … I lived in a flat with nine other people at university, six of them male, and not once did our flat look as grotesquely dirty as this. Neither Mum nor Danielle have so much as looked at an antibacterial wipe or toilet brush since I went on holiday. They have helped themselves to my possessions and treated my property as though it's a squat.

I go downstairs, gripping the handrail tightly to steady myself. Mum looks up at me and smiles.

'You look a bit peaky, Caitlin. Are you sure you won't stay and have a drink? Or are you wanting to get your head down, get rid of the jet lag?'

One woman nods at Chris and whoops, 'I'd like to get my head down on him!' Oh piss off, you perimenopausal, nicotine-addicted harridan.

I tell them, 'You have to go. I need to speak to Mum alone.' Instantly the mood sours and they turn to Mum like a pack of vociferous little terriers: *Are you going to let her speak to us like that? Why the hell should we go, you live here too! Let's go out, leave the miserable cow to tidy up.*

Mum, as usual, shrinks from the conflict. She is visibly deflating, like a punctured balloon. Her eyes meet mine, mutely appealing for me to step in and make them cease their clamour. I throw her a lifeline.

My eyes sweep the room, making contact with each and every one of her guests.

'Get. Out. Of. My. House.' They go, gathering up their bags and coats and complaining loudly. One of them reaches for an unopened bottle of champagne on the sideboard, a bottle that Chris bought me to celebrate our six-month anniversary. I lean over and close my hand about the neck of the bottle, then give her my best death stare. She quickly lets go.

They depart, slamming the door petulantly on their way

out. Mum stands there, looking after them, and then she bursts into tears. I fold my arms across my chest.

'What the hell was that?' I demand.

'I volunteer with one of them at the charity shop. She invited me to bingo, we went for a few drinks and they just sort of invited themselves here. I couldn't think of how to ask them to leave. Thank goodness you're back!' She approaches me, arms outstretched for an embrace. I take a step back, and her face falls.

'Look at what you've done to my house!' I exclaim, pointing to a brown, circular burn on the arm of my sofa. The sofa that I bought brand new, less than a year ago.

'We can clean it up.'

'I know we can clean it up! That's not the point! This is my home as well as yours, and you've turned it into an absolute shit tip. Furniture, towels, bedding, all stuff I bought and paid for, ruined! You've helped yourself to my food, my clothes, my make-up, and you've not tidied or cleaned up after yourself. I give up my work space, I share my bed so that you can both live here, and you treat this place like a dosshouse!'

Chris has been standing silently, watching. Now he comes over and lays a placating hand on my arm.

'It won't be like this for much longer,' he murmurs. I shake my head, blinking away furious tears. Mum might have stopped self-harming, but she's reverted back to her slovenly, lazy habits. I know that this is not an aberration; this mound of dusty, grease-encrusted filth was the house I grew up in. Will Social Services even let Dani live with her in such disgusting, unsanitary conditions?

I turn and point accusingly at the cat, who stops licking its arse and stares back at me disdainfully.

'I mean, you bought a cat! You know I'm allergic! Look what it's doing to me!' I mop at my eyes.

'Dani found it trapped in a wheelie bin,' she says helplessly. 'We adopted it. We couldn't just leave it there, could we?'

'Take it to the abandoned animal shelter!'

She picks up the beast and chucks it under the chin. 'We couldn't do that to Mr Eccles, could we? We couldn't just abandon a poor fluffy little kitty,' she croons, scratching behind his ears.

'Why not? You had no problem doing it to your daughter!' Both she and Chris look startled. She lowers the cat to the ground gently. 'I'm sorry,' I say. 'I didn't mean that.' I'm not sorry, not really, because I'm only telling the truth. She did hand me over to Social Services and do a runner. But I try to take the words back because I sense she's losing control, and I don't want to push her over the edge.

She looks around the room, her eyes widening as though she's seeing for the first time the mess she's made and the chaos she's caused. I stand, looking at the floor, feeling very strongly that there's something else which needs to be said, but I can't quite put my finger on it ...

'Where's Dani?' I ask.

'Staying with a friend.' Her voice quivers, betraying her uncertainty. She doesn't know where Dani is. Why am I not in the least surprised?

'Which friend?' I ask.

'Tony.'

'With an i or a y?' She shrugs helplessly. How is she supposed to know? 'You met this person before you let Dani stay with them? Please tell me you've spoken to their parents?' She shakes her head, a bewildered expression creeping across her face as though it never occurred to her that she might need to do that.

'When will she be home?'

'I ... I ...'

'When was the last time you saw her?'

'Before I went to bingo … the morning … no … it was the day before that. Thursday evening, I think. It's all a bit hazy.'

'Forty-eight hours ago?' I pull out my mobile and hit speed dial. Danielle's number goes straight to voicemail. I hang up and immediately redial. Again, voicemail. I try a third time.

'Has she put anything on social media?' Chris suggests. 'Could you contact her online?'

I open up my apps and view Dani's profiles. It corresponds with Mum's timeframe. Her last post was a comment on Facebook, 49 hours ago. Nothing at all since then. I look up at him.

'I'm going to have to phone the police, aren't I?' He nods.

Mum's hand goes to her mouth. 'I didn't think …' she says, in that same helpless tone of voice.

I turn and scream in her face, 'No, you didn't! How can you call yourself a mother? You are BEYOND REDEMPTION!' It takes every ounce of my self-control not to slap her stupid, useless, irresponsible face. At that moment I don't care about her mental health or a possible relapse. All I care about is Dani's safety.

She bursts into tears, but I turn my back on her, ignore her sobs and dial 101. As we wait for an officer to attend we go about the house, looking for clues as to where Dani may have gone. Her toothbrush and hair straighteners are missing, suggesting she was planning an overnight stay.

I log on to all my social media and post a message on Dani's pages and profiles, tagging her and her closest friends, urging them to contact us. I message several of her mates directly and ask when was the last time they saw her, do they know where she was staying last night?

Then I phone Mrs Court, who luckily for me, happens to be in school. She rings me back once she's accessed her class lists for the next academic year, and confirms that there is no one called Tony, Anthony, Toni, Antonia or Tonya or any variant of the name, registered at St. Luke's. There's only one Tony, and he's coming up into Year 7, so Dani can't possibly have met him.

Chris scans Danielle's various online accounts, checking to see whether she has anybody called Toni/y as a friend or follower. She has nearly a thousand friends on Facebook, but not one of that name.

I even try to hack into her accounts myself, to see if there are any messages about her overnight stay. Her friends begin to reply, saying that they'd expected her to go shopping with them on Saturday lunchtime, but she'd messaged them all, saying simply: CHANGE OF PLAN. C U NEXT WEEK BABES XXXX. I question them about possible boyfriends, men she may have mentioned, even potential girlfriends. They all say the same thing: she had a crush on Benjamin in Year 11, but he wasn't interested. They can't suggest who she may have stayed with last night.

At this point I'm fearing that the answer is only to be found via her private messages, and that she's fallen prey to a cunning online predator. By the time the police arrive I am pacing the living room, kicking pizza boxes and dirty clothes out of the way. I'm ready to start punching the walls.

When the police arrive I speak to them outside. Mum, the last person to see Dani, is being about as useful as a chocolate fireguard. She can't remember what Dani was wearing or carrying, can't remember anything beyond a vague 'She was planning to stay over with Toni/y.' She flits about, wringing her hands and wailing. It's like having a bloody wasp in the room.

The police depart, promising to do their very best to find Dani and bring her home. Chris makes us all a cup of tea, and I briefly fantasise about throwing it back in his face. How can he drink tea, when Dani has been missing for two whole days? I can't sit still. I stalk across the living room like a caged animal driven insane by years of captivity. Occasionally I go upstairs to stare at the pile of clothes at the foot of our bed, as though they are runes which might offer clues as to my sister's whereabouts. The clothes remain mute, but my imagination has gone into overdrive. Images flash through my head: Dani lying beneath a pile of bin bags in some side street, Dani being humped by some lecherous paedophile she met online, Dani stranded miles from home after being mugged, cold and alone on some station platform …

'I'm going out to look for her,' I announce, snatching up my car keys.

'I'll come with you,' Chris and Mum declare simultaneously. I look from one face to the other. It's like that riddle with the fox, the grain and the chicken. I have to leave one of them at home, in case Dani returns unexpectedly. Chris is a steadying influence, and will be useful muscle if Dani is found in the clutches of a man … but if I leave Mum at home she's likely to do something stupidly reckless. We are both driven by the same harmful, destructive impulse – except that it's in my nature to lash out, and hers to turn it inwards. We both need to channel our energy into action, or else destroy something.

'Chris, stay here. Mum get in the car, keep your eyes peeled, and don't speak to me unless you see Dani.'

We start by combing the area near our house, methodically driving up and down residential streets. Occasionally, we stop and show a photo of Dani to an observant-looking dog walker or a gang of kids. They all answer in the negative. Slowly we widen our search, visiting places Dani has previously mentioned: places I know kids from St. Luke's hang out, and places I used to frequent myself. When it gets too dark to spot her from the car I drive to the town centre and walk up and down the high street, showing her photo to every doorman, bar tender or off-licence server, in the hope that one of them will have spotted her trying to sneak in with a boyfriend. None of them have seen her. Some of them offer to share her details with contacts further afield. By 11pm her disappearance has gone viral: over 100 people have shared the police post asking after her whereabouts, and another 100 have shared my original request for information. If she has access to the internet, she must be aware that we are looking for her.

I'm all for heading over to Chester or Wrexham, but at a quarter to midnight Mum takes me by the shoulders and says, 'Caitlin, you're exhausted … You shouldn't be behind the wheel. If the police see you driving they will pull you over.' I realise that she's right. My brain is too frazzled to calculate the time difference between here and the Seychelles, or to work out how many hours I've been awake. All I know is that it feels like a long, long, long time since I was last asleep.

I walk towards the car. I feel light-headed, almost drunk with tiredness. Mum catches up with me and takes the car keys out of my hand. I'm surprised by this, because I can't ever recall her driving. She assures me that she's had a license for almost twenty years, it's just that she's never owned a car. She guides me towards the passenger side of the vehicle, buckles me in and turns on the warm air blowers. The warmth envelopes me, the movement of the car lulls me, and I can no longer fight the urge to asleep. A few minutes' shut-eye and I'll be ready to look for Dani again …

21

The click-click-click of the indicator is the first thing I hear, like a mechanical heartbeat echoing my own. I open my eyes to find that I'm still in the car and Mum is still in the driver's seat, although the car is stationary. She has me by the shoulder and is shaking me gently. I feel something on my thigh, buzzing like a matchbox full of wasps.

'Caitlin, Caitlin, your phone is ringing …' I retrieve my phone from my pocket just as the ringing ends. I swipe the screen and a message appears: 1 MISSED CALL. DANI.

I hit the redial button, my heart racing. She answers immediately.

'Dani, where are you? Are you okay?'

She whispers her reply, her words barely audible.

'Cat … I'm at Dad's.'

'Are you okay?'

'He's been drinking. I've never seen him like this before. Please come and get me.' I hear a muffled thump and some semi-coherent words. He's talking to himself, as he was wont to do when I lived at home. Several nights he fell through the front door in the company of his invisible friends, pontificating to thin air. In his head he was still at the pub. You had to tiptoe around him as though he was a sleepwalker, and at all costs you had to avoid startling him.

'Dani, where are you?'

'I'm in his bathroom. I've locked the door.'

'Good. Stay in there, we'll be right over. What's his address?'

She gives the address of a town further down the coast; a miserable land of bedsits and fly-tipping. I know of the street but am unsure of its precise location, so I program it into the GPS on my phone.

'Let's go and get her,' I tell Mum, but on hearing Dani's voice she has come over all of a dither. She keeps trying to signal to move off, but ends up stalling the engine and repeatedly hitting the windscreen wipers. They wave maniacally at us, screeching as dry rubber scrapes dry glass.

'Move over, I'll drive,' I snap. She gets out of the car and races around the bonnet; I hop over the gearstick into the driver's seat. As we drive to our destination I realise that I really should have brought Chris. Mum will be of no practical use in getting Dani out of Dad's drunken clutches. I will have to do it alone.

'I had no idea she was in contact with him … no idea … I can't understand why she went to see him … Do you know why, Caitlin? I can't think why she would want to see him … I mean, why would she go and visit him, after all he did?' She's like a stuck record, parroting the same disbelief over and over again, until I want to punch the steering wheel and scream at her to shut the fucking fuck up.

Dad's new home is in a narrow cul-de-sac of terraced houses. It's a forbidding place, heavy curtains keeping the entire ground floor shrouded in a gothic darkness. The tiny yard is fronted by a spiked fence: Vlad the Impaler's seaside bolthole. I park outside and kill the engine.

Danielle said they were in 15A, so presumably the house has been divided into two dwellings. I guess that Dad inhabits the ground floor.

'Stay here,' I tell Mum. 'If I'm not out in five minutes, phone the police.' I'm banking on Dad being so inebriated that this will be a smash-and-grab extraction. I'll be in and out before he's even realised that I'm in the flat with him. No police, no confrontation, no arguments or stand-offs – it will be less dangerous for all involved – providing I don't screw up. If I can't get to her then we will have no choice but to get the police involved, and from experience I know that will get messy. Dani once let it slip that when he was arrested for assaulting me it took four cops to get the handcuffs on him. He was carried out of the house wearing restraints and a spit hood, screaming threats about frying bacon.

Slowly, slowly, I ease open the wrought iron gate. There are flagstones, but thankfully, no gravel underfoot. The front door leads to flat 15B. I open the side gate, rattling the latch as little as humanly possible, and am confronted with a blaze of light and a sign saying 15A. A narrow window is illuminated, but the pane is frosted to conceal its occupant. I creep towards the light and squint through the glass. Dad has lost most of his hair, but the amorphous blob visible through the distorting glass is a pale brown, the same shade as Dani's mousy hair. Ever so gently, I tap on the window. Seconds later the shape rears up, and the little ventilation window at the top is pushed open. I'm only a little over five foot, much too small to reach the top of the window; but when I see Dani's hand pushed through the opening I step onto a waste water pipe, haul myself up and catch at her fingers. She squeezes my hand, tightly.

'Cat!' I can hear from the tone of her voice that she's been crying. 'Get me out of here!'

'Has he hurt you?'

'No, but he won't let me go. He says he'll hurt me if I try to go home.'

'Can you get to the door?'

'He's locked it. He says I can't leave, he doesn't want to die alone.'

You miserable prick. If there is a hell, I hope it's teetotal. I hope hell is one long Alcoholics Anonymous meeting. No, I hope hell is a free bar, and you are chained to a water cooler of dog's piss, forced to watch everybody you hate drinking perpetually and enjoying themselves ...

I won't be able to get to her on my own. 'Dani, stay in the toilet and keep the door locked. I'm going to phone the police.

Hang in there, I'll be right back …' I drop down to the floor. Her fingers grab frantically at thin air.

'Don't leave me!' she begs.

'I'm still here Dani, you're not alone.' I reach into my pocket for my phone and dial 999. As the operator asks, 'What's your emergency?' the side door of the building opens. Before I even have a chance to consider whether I should end the call or try to stay on the line, something heavy coshes me over the head and my mobile phone clatters to the floor. I regain my balance quickly and go to retrieve it, only for a trainer-shod foot to kick it out of my reach. The accuracy of that kick worries me. It's almost worthy of Aaron Ramsey. I straighten up and find myself looking at Dad. Straight away I can smell the booze on his breath. He reeks familiarly of cheap, stomach-rotting cider. Worryingly, his tolerance must have increased over the years, because in spite of his boozy stench he's steady on his feet and seemingly in control of all his faculties. His aim was good. I reach up and touch the crown of my head. Where I was struck throbs painfully, but my hair is dry and my scalp intact.

'Thought you was a burglar,' he says, as though that justifies the assault. 'You really shouldn't be poking about down people's back alleys.' He jerks his head towards the open door, indicating that I am to enter. I obey, knowing that if I can keep him calm and talking for four minutes, Mum will phone the police. If I can prevent the situation from escalating for another ten or fifteen minutes, there should be a knock on the door. All I have to do is keep my temper, and avoid provoking his.

Once inside, he bolts the door and slides the chain into place.

'Long time, daughter. Except I can't really call you that now, can I?'

'No more than I can call you Dad,' I say, struggling to keep my voice from quivering. It's been six years since I saw him in person, standing in the dock in his cheap supermarket suit. I have to take a deep breath and remind myself that I'm no longer the teenager he drunkenly terrorised.

'Have a drink with me, for old time's sake,' he offers, going to the fridge and removing two cans of Special Brew. He tosses one to me and I manage to catch it. It hisses and spits as I open it. 'Cheers.'

His mouth cracks into a smile, revealing that several of his front teeth are missing. The others jut out of his mouth like gravestones sunk into marshy ground. His face is deeply lined, the eyes are bloodshot, the smile mirthless. I know he's five years older than Mum, but you'd take him for someone ready to claim his state pension.

I hold my can aloft and declare ironically, '*Iechyd da.*'

'Iacky da. You're taking the piss now.'

'I don't understand.' Of course I do, but I want to keep him talking. He takes the bait.

'Sit down and I'll tell you.' He turns and walks into the living room, clearly expecting me to follow him. As he passes the bathroom door he bangs on the painted white wood of the door and yells, 'Danielle, your sister's here. Stop hiding in the bathroom. Come and say hello.'

Dani emerges, her eyes red with crying and her skin ashen with fear. She grabs my hand, squeezing it as though she never intends to let go.

The front room is an ugly shithole, befitting my ugly shit of a father. Its walls are a grubby white, with heavy velour curtains at the windows to block out all traces of the outside world. A bare lightbulb hangs from the ceiling, the Artex patterned with swirls of black mould. A dusty green armchair sits in the bay window, a matching but battered two-seater sofa against the opposite wall. That is all the furniture in the room, and the rolled-up sleeping bag in the corner suggests it may well double as a bed. Perhaps Dani has slept here. How long has she been visiting Dad in secret?

Dad sits in the armchair. We both perch on the sofa, squashed tightly together. I can feel her body trembling. Dad begins the conversation in an easy, almost pleasant tone, betraying no sign of the aggression which caused him to smash a bottle over the back of my skull only moments earlier. I've seen his dangerously unpredictable rage at work many times. Better than anyone, I know the random acts of savage violence he is capable of.

He returned home from the pub one evening to find that I'd fallen asleep on the sofa. Drunk and angry that Mum had locked the bedroom door, he came downstairs and threw me to the floor. Confused and startled at being awoken from a deep sleep, I cried out and resisted. For that, he slammed me into the coffee table and punched me and kicked me until I felt my ribs crack. When I curled up into a defensive ball he grabbed my ankle, dragged me a few feet into the kitchen and left me lying on the floor. I lay there, perfectly still, until I heard him snoring on the sofa. I played dead and choked back my sobs of pain to stop him from killing me.

The gloves cannot come off. No matter what he says, for our safety, I cannot let him provoke me.

He leers, 'You've come to have one last butchers before I croak it.'

'The only reason I'm here is to collect Dani and take her back to Mum. She's worried sick.'

He raises the can to his lips and gulps greedily like a horse at a trough, then wipes his mouth with the sleeve of his sweater.

'Don't give me that. She doesn't know where Dani is half the time. She's been visiting me for weeks. Your Mum's too bloody lazy to care.' Another gulp, and he gazes into the empty fireplace, a vacant look in his eyes. 'When you were two or three, Caitlin, she left the back door open and you got out into the street. Too busy watching TV to realise you'd done a runner. I caught you just as you were about to run into the traffic. My biggest regret is that I stopped you from running.' He talks as though he's regretting not buying a timeshare in Marbella, rather than wishing death on a child he raised as his own. It would be disturbing, if I'd not grown used to his illogical emotional abuse over the years.

'I'm not here to talk about me,' I tell him, keeping my voice quiet and level as though I'm talking to a difficult student. My firm-but-fair teacher voice, devoid of any emotion. 'I'm here to collect Danielle and take her home. This isn't about me.' He drains and discards the can, crushing it so easily that I wince at the memory of his fingers bruising my flesh, twisting it in his vice-like grip.

'Oh, but it's all about *you.*' He points towards me as though I'm an exhibit at the circus and should be bathed in a drum roll and spotlights. 'You, Caitlin, are the problem. This is your fault. Neither of us wanted a baby, see, but along you came, and we tried to do the right thing. What a bloody mistake that turned out to be. Her depression started once you were born. I should have made her have an abortion, put you up for adoption before she got attached.' Dani gasps at the malice of his words, and I remember that she knows nothing of my bastardy.

'Don't worry, he's not talking about both of us,' I reassure her quietly.

'Our Dani's a good girl, not like you. Her coming along is what saved our marriage.' I almost spit out my drink at this comment, but I want to get us out of here in one piece, so I force down the mouthful of his bile-flavoured piss water and manage to retain my composure. Irony never was Dad's strong point. I manage to relax my face into an expressionless mask, my best poker face, and imagine that I'm listening politely to the drunken bullshit ramblings of the local bar fly.

Dad gets up and goes to the kitchen, retrieves another can from the fridge. He downed his first can in a little under three minutes. Keep going at this rate and there's a chance that he'll pass out before the police even get here.

Dani looks up at him pleadingly. 'Dad, please don't be like this ...'

'Sorry sweetheart, but your sister needs to know what your mum's really like. It's about time she heard the truth about darling Mummy, the poor, sick victim. She's living with you, isn't she?' I nod in reply. 'You're a bloody fool. Do you think she loves you?' Leaning against the door jamb, he looks down on me and continues spitting his bile. 'Did you ever wonder why she spent so much time hidden away in her room? It was because she couldn't stand the sight of you. I'll bet she never told you this, but she was happy when the Social took you off our hands. We were happy, me and Danielle and your Mum, we were a proper family without you. I came out of prison and moved straight back home. She didn't blame me for what happened.'

I think back to what Mum said to me, a day or two before her suicide attempt: *I was scared of him, too scared to leave. He would have found us, Caitlin. He told me so many times that he would kill me if I left. I had to let you go.*

'She was scared to leave you. You threatened to kill her.'

'Is that what she said?' He seems almost amused. 'Of course it is. I'm the big bad wolf. I'll bet she told you all sorts of lies to make you feel sorry for her. She's a parasite, a fucking user who doesn't give a damn about anyone other than herself. I should have got out years ago. I would have, but for my Danielle.' He smiles at Dani, trying to look like the doting papa, but she looks at her feet and refuses to meet his gaze.

Whatever her reason for resuming contact with him, it's pretty obvious that she's regretting it now.

He's probably been storing this revelation up for years. This is his silver-tipped bullet, his last attempt to wound me. He's probably expecting me to feel betrayed and bitter, but the thing is, I know that he's right. Actions speak louder than words, and Mum turned a blind eye to his drink-fuelled beatings. She stayed away from court and refused to testify against him. She was a shit mother, and even now, even though she professes regret, her current actions tell me that she is still a shit mother.

However, as Chris would say, there are three sides to every story: yours, mine, and the truth. Mum is such a piss poor excuse for a parent that she barely deserves the title, but that doesn't mean that she wasn't bullied and coerced into obeying Dad. He knew that she was sick and vulnerable, and used her depression as a weapon against her. For years he hung on to her with the tenacity of a lock-jawed pit bull. He's telling me all of this because her parental guilt, the desire to redeem herself as a mother, is the one part of Mum that he's never managed to subdue or destroy. He's telling me all this imagining that he's shattering some burgeoning, gossamer thin mother-daughter bond. He wants to hurt me one last time.

But I'm done with both of them, with their selfishness, their wilful self-destruction and their toxicity. Dad tries to place the blame for their collective dysfunction on my shoulders, but their mistakes and problems are not my fault. They can rearrange deck chairs on the Titanic. I intend to sit back and watch from the comfort of my iceberg, with Dani at my side.

I get to my feet and my sister rises with me, still clinging to my hand.

'Blame me for ruining your marriage if you want. Blame me for your alcoholism too, if it makes you feel better. But the truth is that you and Mum decided to bring me into the world and be responsible for a child, and you fucked up, big time.

You destroyed my childhood, but I'm not going to let you ruin Dani's. She's not staying here to watch you drink yourself into an early grave. We're going now, and you won't stop us. The police are on their way, and we are leaving.'

Dad looks at his daughter, the little princess who managed to avoid his ire. 'Dani sweet, you promised you wouldn't leave me here. I'm your parent as much as she is, I have a right to see you ...' Dani's eyes are still fixed on the floor. She can't look him in the eyes. Whether it's from guilt or fear, I can't say.

'If you want to leave, Dani, just go. He can't stop you.' I tell her calmly. She takes a step back and lets go of my hand.

'You're not leaving,' Dad spits. In the blink of an eye, he has changed. A monster rears its head, rage bristling like a mane. The glazed expression in his eyes is gone, replaced by a cold and steely anger. I remember that look well.

Dani takes another step back, although her eyes are now wide with fear and fixed on him. She knows what's coming next.

'I'm sorry, Dad, but I want to go home,' she bleats. With that, she turns and dashes to the back door. At the rattle of the key in the lock, Dad springs into life.

'I said, you're not going!' he snarls, covering the living room floor in just two strides. Dani screams and retreats further back into the kitchen, cowering against a unit. Instinctively, I sidestep and place myself in Dad's path. He pushes my shoulders, tries to barge me out of the way. I step backwards to stop myself from stumbling, but feel my body stiffen, muscles tightening, fingers curling into fists. I'm not going anywhere. I'm not moving for him. We're almost nose to nose, eyeballing one another. I can taste his sour breath. Back down now and he'll pounce. I roll my shoulders with a boxer's swagger, tower over him, look down on him in spite of the fact that I'm only five foot two. Tom and Geoffrey were sparring partners. This is the main event.

'Get out of here, Dani,' I keep my gaze locked onto Dad's. I hear the door handle rattling; feel a blast of midnight air on the back of my neck, and I know that she's gone. She's safe. The same, unfortunately, cannot be said of me.

Dad is staring over my shoulder, at the space where Dani stood only seconds before. I see a flicker in his eyes, a twitch of the mouth indicating sorrow or regret. He knows that he won't see Dani again. His attempts to poison her against her mum had the opposite effect to the one he intended – it has scared her away.

He turns his attention back to me, and I realise that in staying to observe his moment of regret I've missed my own cue to escape. Looking at him, I'm reminded of a Gaboon viper I saw at Chester Zoo. It was a thick, slovenly-looking snake, but its baleful, cold eyes warned me that I would be foolish to underestimate its speed and venom. Even behind a pane of glass it made my flesh crawl. My flesh is crawling now, and there is no pane of glass to protect me.

'She was the last thing I had to live for,' he says. 'All I had left.' I hear the can drop from his fingers and clatter onto the floor, landing somewhere between our feet. I flinch at the noise, and he smirks. Then he headbutts me, nutting me right on the nose. I stagger backwards, blinded as the centre of my face explodes and my sinuses are swamped with a searing pain. I clutch at my nose, blinking the tears from my eyes. As I straighten up, regain my vision and prepare for the next punch, I become aware that Dad is no longer in front of me. I turn and see that he has moved into the kitchen. He's yanking drawers open, rattling the cutlery in its tray. The blade flashes in his hand, a vegetable knife, small and vicious. This is not going to be a fair fight. Adrenalin floods my veins, heightening every sense to an almost unbearable level. I seem to feel every inch of skin and every nerve quivering in expectation of the knife's cutting edge. My heart is racing, the hairs on my arms standing up: *Get out. Now.*

I dive through the side door, stubbing my toe on the wooden frame. I know I'm hurt as I can feel myself limping, but I feel no pain as I run down the side alley and yank the gate open. He's behind me, he's on my tail, his footfall a nanosecond behind my own, only a hair's breadth separating us. Dani has left the wrought iron gate open. I run through and yank it closed without looking back. The gate is stiff, and Dad pausing to open it will buy me the fraction of a second I need to get into the car … The handle of the car door is within my reach, in my grasp, raised up and the door is open and I'm in, I'm in, I'm in and the door is locked behind me.

'Oh hell, oh hell, oh hell …' I pant, as I fumble for the keys and start the engine.

'Go!' shrieks Mum, as Dad's heavy palm comes down against the roof of the car. He rattles my door handle, and for a heart-stopping second I wonder whether or not I have central locking. Dani and Mum clearly have the same thought, as they both dive to their respective doors and press down on the locking mechanism, even though I do indeed have central locking and all the doors are already locked.

I stamp down on the clutch and find first gear. As I turn the wheel, instinctively glancing in the rear-view mirror, I feel something strike the car. I turn and look over my shoulder, just as a brick strikes the nearside rear window for a second time. The glass shatters into a cobweb, but the pane remains intact. With Dani's petrified screams piercing my ears, I jump on the accelerator and we lurch forwards. The engine stalls. In a panic I twist the key in the ignition again and again, not realising that I've restarted the car until Mum shrieks, 'It's on! It's on!' Pulling away, I almost clip the bumper of the car in front of me. I see a flash of reddish brown strike my own window, cracking the glass right down the middle.

I almost heave a sigh of relief; until I remember that we're in a cul-de-sac, and getting out of here will mean turning around and driving straight past Dad. We stop at the bottom of the road. I consider trying to reverse straight back up the street, but it's narrow and there are cars parked on either side. I begin a three-point turn, cursing the Victorian builders who didn't foresee the need for off-road parking. My heart is racing as though it's about to explode out of my rib cage like a face-hugger. I'm painfully aware that I'm hemmed in by parked cars and that while I struggle not to prang any of them, Dad may be moving closer and closer. After a few horrible seconds I manage to turn the car around so that we are facing the exit.

Dani has wedged herself between mine and Mum's seats. Her eyes dart side-to-side wildly, scanning the street for any sign of him. We sit for a second in total silence. When the ambush doesn't come, Dani begins to whimper.

'Cat, let's go!' she begs. I press the accelerator flat to the floor. The pathetic 1.2 litre engine of my car lets out a roar of protest, but it obeys my command and springs forward. The main road is in sight and I know in which direction the police station lies. I've been there enough times.

There's barely even time to register Dad's presence as he steps off the pavement, arm raised to strike. His bulk hits the bonnet in a puppet-like flail of arms and legs. It happens at lightning speed, but one instant imprints itself onto my mind with a sickening clarity: his head striking the windscreen. By the time we skid to a halt he is already gone, leaving only a bloody smear on the glass, inches from my nose. I sit rigid, my knuckles white from gripping the steering wheel. There's a moment of silence, the breath frozen in our throats. Then Danielle lets out the most piercing, wordless scream I've ever heard. Mum twists in her seat, catches at her arms and begs her to calm down, but the screaming goes on and on, undulating like a car alarm. Lights begin to appear in the windows of neighbouring houses.

I unfasten my seatbelt and step out of the car, taking Mum's phone with me. For the second time that night I dial 999.

I tell the operator, 'I've run someone over.'

Someone has come out of one of the properties. They are speaking to me, but it's indistinct, as though I'm hearing them from a great distance. They take the phone from my hand, perhaps realising that I'm in no fit state to be triaging Dad or dealing with the emergency services.

I'm staring down at my father, who is lying in the middle of the road. He's dead, and I am the one who killed him. The laugh escapes like a hiccup. The next one is like a convulsion. I clap a hand over my mouth to stifle the hysterical scream building up within me.

He's dead, and the person who drove a car into him happens to be the daughter he disowned; the daughter suspended many times from school for getting into fights; the daughter who was arrested and nearly prosecuted for assault; suspended from her job after accusations of misconduct; the daughter who has spent months attending therapy and anger management. Open my book and its pages are printed with hatred towards him. I've seen the lengths barristers will go to in order to blacken a name. Nobody, nobody in a jury is going to believe that this was an accident. I had a motive to kill him; once I dreamt of doing so. Perhaps two or three years ago I would have considered doing it.

This time it will go to trial. I'm going to jail, for manslaughter at the very least. I'm going to prison, and not just for six months, but for years …

Blue lights and sirens, too late for either of us. I can't hold the screams back. Someone, a stranger, puts their arms around me and holds me against their shoulder, imagining that I'm hysterical over the accident. I push them away and carry on screaming in anguish for the life I've barely begun to live, the life I can see bleeding out before my eyes. I finally understand the hopelessness Mum must experience: bitter, black, blinding and stupefying. There is no way out. It's like soil filling my mouth, claws grabbing at me and dragging me down to a place where there is no light and no air.

Blue lights. Uniforms. Crackling walkie talkies. They've sent the whole team: police, ambulance, fire engine. All this for Dad, and he's dead. They're just here to do the clearing up. Put us both in boxes. He's dead. I might as well be.

'Caitlin,' I feel a pair of arms go about me, light as a bird's bones. Mum is cradling me in her arms, stroking my hair. 'It's going to be all right,' she whispers, her mouth warm against my ear. 'I promise, it's going to be all right.'

'It won't …' I moan. 'Look at him. Look at what I've done to him …' Then she cups my face in her hands and draws me close, so that I'm looking into her ink dark eyes.

'Hush,' she murmurs, then she glances over her shoulder at Dani, beckoning her to join us. She puts an arm over each of our shoulders and draws us both close. We grow calmer in her embrace. For a second we hold one another tightly, heads bowed, weeping. How different would our lives have been, if we'd held one another like this from the start?

'I did it.' Mum's voice is so quiet that we both freeze, unsure if we're hearing her correctly. Dani raises her eyes to mine in query. Mum continues in a whisper: 'You tell the police exactly what happened; except that I was in the driver's seat.'

'No!' wails Dani tearfully. 'No! They'll send you to …'

'I know. But if Caitlin goes to prison and I get sick again, who's going to look after you?' Dani grabs at Mum's sleeve.

'You can't tell them, you can't! We'll tell them … we'll …' She looks from Mum to me and back to Mum again, and the realisation dawns on her that one of us is going to have to pay for this. She bursts into tears again – huge, silent body-shaking sobs. Mum slides a hand into her soft hair and plants a kiss on her forehead with an air of finality that is like a knife to my heart.

'I won't let you take the fall …' I begin, but she interrupts, the sight of an approaching policeman making her urgent.

'You will, and you'll look after Dani for me.' She smiles, and in spite of the hell of the moment I can see that the prospect of this is genuinely giving her some comfort. 'My girls, my girls, look after one another.' Mum kisses me. Her lips leave their moist, love-shaped mark on my cheek. There isn't time for me to return the gesture or even embrace her. She turns to the approaching policeman.

'Officer, I'm afraid that I may have killed my husband.'

Dani lets out a fresh squeal of grief. I hold her close, rocking her wordlessly. I'm torn. Every bit of honesty and decency screams out that I should step forward and take Mum's place, tell the truth and hope they believe it was all an accident … But then Mum looks back over her shoulder at me, and she smiles, she actually smiles at me. She's not afraid.

'Don't worry!' she calls as the police officer leads her towards the waiting squad car. Another police officer comes over to see if we're okay. We both nod, dumbly.

'You're probably both in shock,' he says, kindly. Shock, yes, but also fear is keeping our mouths closed. He tells us that at some point they will need statements from both of us as to what happened.

'Will we have to go down to the police station?' asks Dani, her eyes seeming to swell up and fill her face. She looks like a bush baby confronted by a tooth-filled predator, and I know why: lying to the police, lying on tape recorder, lying when you're in the depths of a police station, is not as easy as lying at the roadside. The officer senses her fear, but interprets it as fear of authority rather than discovery. He reassures her that it will be nothing like being arrested and that she has nothing to be afraid of.

Looking at the tears swimming in her eyes, I realise that Mum and I are asking Dani to do something awful. I'm not sure whether it counts as perjury, but it is certainly dishonesty. I don't know whether she'll be able to stand the strain, or the guilt. For all I know, once the shock fades she might turn against me – after all, I did just kill her father. What if she doesn't go along with Mum's plan? It's both risky and unfair to expect her to go along with the story. Mum has made a noble gesture, but I can't accept it. I can't let her …

'Caitlin?' I look up to see a firefighter, but I have to take a few steps closer and look at the face underneath his helmet before I recognise him as Drew, Chris' watch manager.

'Drew!' I cry. He gestures to my car.

'Is this yours? Were you involved?'

Before I can answer, somebody calls, 'We've got a pulse!'

I see a paramedic with a defibrillator in hand, and two others in their fluorescent coats standing by, stretcher and neck collar at the ready. The feeling returns, as though soil is seeping into my lungs, as though my head is being crammed full of earth until it's ready to explode. I try to take a deep breath and steady myself, but white lights begin to dance in front of my eyes. My head hits the tarmac, and a pain momentarily explodes across the side of my face, before the world goes black.

Three hours later and I'm sitting in a cubicle in A&E, waiting for a doctor to sign my discharge papers. Our phones have been seized as possible evidence by the police, so Dani has gone off in search of a payphone. I sit with my head in my hands, taking deep, slow breaths to try and fight the panic rising like flames inside my chest. I close my eyes tightly, trying to detach myself from the situation. I hear Karen's voice telling me: 'Don't give me feelings, Caitlin. Give me *facts.*' Okay, facts, I can do this. I can break this nightmare down into manageable, factual bullet points and repeat them to the police ... No, I can't. I close my eyes, but all I can see is his blood on the pavement like a vermillion halo, his eyes were open and unblinking like those of a snake, his hair matted with gore ...

The memory causes the bile to rise and the guilt to wash over me, hot as fever. I grab the little cardboard basin the nurse gave me and cradle it against my stomach, fighting the urge to be sick. Dani swishes back the curtain, enters the cubicle and stops, frowning disapprovingly.

'You can't discharge yourself, Cat. The doctor said so. You're not well enough to go home.' I'm a trembling, tearful mess, alternating between hot and cold shivers and bouts of nausea. I know that she and the doctor are right – I am not ready to go home. But it's okay, because I have no intention of going home. I stand up and reach for my coat.

'I am discharging myself, then I'm going to the police station. If I come clean now, they might not do us for perverting the course of justice, or whatever it is ...'

'Sit down,' says Dani, firmly. I continue putting on my coat, although suddenly it doesn't have any arm holes, and the hood seems to be somewhere near the hem. 'Sit the hell down!' she hisses, pulling the coat away from me. 'You suffered a head injury, you're in shock, and you're shaking so much you can't even get yourself dressed. You are not going to the bloody police station while you're like this!'

'I have to!' I say, not bothering to lower my voice. 'It's guilt that's making me feel like this. I'll be okay ...'

'Who do you think you are, Lady Bloody Macbeth?' I hear Dad's impatience in her voice. She perches on the chair at my side and hisses, 'You *have* to promise, Cat. You have to promise me that we'll keep quiet about what happened, like Mum wants us to.'

'How can I? Do you expect me to lie to the police, to the courts, to Chris, to everyone?' She throws up her hands in frustration, tears of rage welling in her eyes.

'Damn right, I expect you to lie! Listen, I know this is serious shit. It's a crime. But I'm still going to do it. I'm going along with Mum's story, even if she ends up behind bars, because I can't take what will happen if you tell the truth ...' She blinks and the tears spill down her cheeks. She wipes them away impatiently, smearing her mascara. 'If you go to prison, Cat, it's all over. Mum will go back to how she used to be, and when she relapses I won't be able to save her. She needs you.'

I was thirteen the first time I encountered one of Mum's suicide attempts. I remember finding her slumped over the kitchen table, sobbing that she was going to die. There was an empty packet of paracetamol between her fingers. I filled a glass full of salt water and threatened to stick my fingers down her throat unless she drank it all. I remember watching her vomit into the sink, spewing mangled pig flesh, melted cheese and six perfectly round, undigested tablets into the stainless steel sink.

As clear as a flashback, I remember the gut-churning panic and the breathless free-fall of fear as we waited for the ambulance. I learned how to save her because I had no choice, and I don't ever want Dani to experience that hideous burst of adrenalin, or feel the weight of another person's life on her shoulders.

My sister jumps out of her seat and goes to the window, turns her head to one side and presses her cheek flat against the cold glass – a habit leftover from childhood. Mine was to stick my head into the belly of the washing machine and inhale its soapy, chemical scent. We had precious little of a childhood, and tonight her world is on the verge of collapse.

In that second I realise that she's right – I am the only one who can stop it from disintegrating completely.

I go to her and wrap my arms about her tightly. My head is still spinning, and I'm aware that we are both swaying slightly. She turns and buries her face in my shoulder, allowing the tears and snot to flow freely into my T-shirt.

I remember the promise I made to Dani on the day of the suicide attempt: *If you need me, I'll be there. Always.* I'm all she has left, how could I even consider leaving her?

For her sake, I will lie to the police, will commit perjury and pervert the course of justice. For her, I will endure the guilt which, even now is gnawing my innards like a vicious rodent. Or perhaps that's just Dad's cheap booze, taking its revenge.

22

I awaken with a jolt, disorientated and panic-stricken. The same old dream: me, digging a grave intended for Mum and Dad. But as always, I'm the one who ends up face-first in the ground. Sometimes I feel the clay landing on the back of my neck. It's so vivid that I can almost feel its coldness on my skin. Other nights I'm trapped in a coffin and can hear soil rattling down onto its wood as my mum and dad laugh and shovel earth into the grave.

This is the dream that has haunted me since I was first taken away from my parents. Now, it's back with a vengeance. I've dreamt variations of it almost every night in the six weeks since the accident. I know now that it will never alter, and most probably, it will never go away. Sleep is just another part of my punishment.

I slide out of bed without waking Danielle, and go into the bathroom. Glancing out of the window, I see the first streaks of dawn on the horizon. As I dry my hands I hear the hiss-click of the kettle coming to the boil and switching itself off. Mum must be awake too.

She's heard me moving around and has pre-emptively poured me a black coffee. I join her at the kitchen table, where she is nursing a mug of pine-coloured tea.

'Can't sleep?' I ask. She shakes her head.

'You know, I've been thinking for the past few days what I have on my bucket list – what I'd like to do before I go inside. And what's really sad is that I can't think of anything. I mean, I would like to see you and Chris get married, but I've told you already that you're not to wait. And I'd have liked to see Dani getting her GCSE results, but I know that won't happen either. There's nothing else that I'll really miss doing, apart from sitting in the garden and soaking up the sun.'

'Let's go sit in the back garden now,' I suggest. 'Watch the sun rise.'

We put on our coats and slippers, and taking our mugs with us, we settle onto sun loungers and look up above the solar-panelled roofs of the new builds on the estate, up at the pink and yellow clouds. Such is the luminosity of the dawn light that it reminds me of the neon Staedtler highlighters I coveted as a child.

'What time are you due in court?' I ask Mum.

'Eleven.'

'I'll come with you.' It's a school day, but yesterday Mrs Court suggested that I was looking a bit peaky and might find myself mysteriously stricken with a 24-hour bug. Mum shakes her head vehemently. She has steadfastly forbidden Dani and myself to attend any court proceedings; not that there have been many. She pled guilty to dangerous driving at the first opportunity. She might have avoided a custodial sentence, had it not been for the fact that she was drunk. At the roadside she blew almost twice the legal limit. For that reason she is facing a prison sentence which will undoubtedly be higher than anything I would have served. Even knowing this, she has refused time and time again to let me tell the police the truth. Her response is always the same: 'I wasn't there the last time you stood up in court, and I should have been. Let me do this for you now.'

Mum has never satisfactorily explained where she went in the weeks following Dad's arrest. After some prompting, Dani said that she remembered going to stay for several weeks with an 'auntie', probably a cousin or a friend of Mum's. For a long time I secretly hoped for another revelation, something which could explain her absence. Horrible though it sounds, even an admission of a suicide attempt, even her being sectioned, would be preferable to knowing that she did simply choose to let me go. However she maintains her silence, probably because the truth is so unpalatable that she refuses to hurt me further by offering it up. She's trying her best to make amends for the years of neglect. Taking the blame for me is a noble gesture – but it's not a completely selfless one, nor one I can accept easily.

Many nights I've jerked myself out of sleep in a blind panic. The monster called Guilt sits on my stomach, sending my heart racing and sucking the breath from my lungs. He follows me when I'm awake, sitting between Chris and myself like a reminder of some sleazy one night stand. I worry that I'm going to blurt it out randomly, or turn into a truth-telling somnambulist. Dani may have been scornful when she compared me to Lady Macbeth, but I do worry that the guilt will eventually out itself in one way or another. I've begun to suffer panic attacks, something not even 11Y at their very worst could bring on. I feel permanently on-edge and permanently exhausted because I'm not sleeping properly. I hate that I've concealed this from Chris, hate that I can't talk to anyone about how I feel, but most of all, I hate myself for letting Mum sacrifice herself in this way. She, however, seems to be embracing it as some form of personal redemption. I doubt she thinks of perjury or justice. I often hear her snoring as she sleeps the sleep of the just, while I am wakeful with the dishonesty lying heavily on my conscience.

Mum pours the cold remnants of her tea onto the grass and rises from her lounger with difficulty.

'I'm going to pack,' she announces, and I'm left alone, with only my bitter mug of coffee and the twittering of birds for company.

A hundred times I've found myself listening to her own twittering and wishing that she would just shut the hell up for five minutes. Her newfound, New Age belief in 'breathing out the negative' and 'clearing your chakras' and her unceasing commentary on television programmes used to drive me batshit crazy. Now, I find myself wishing for that old, garrulous version of herself. The self-composed, dignified, eloquent version of Mum unnerves me.

I finish my drink and sit watching the dawn for a few minutes before padding back through the French doors. The first thing that catches my eye is a rectangle of white paper lying on the kitchen worktop. I know what it will say, even before I pick it up.

She's walking towards the bus stop at the bottom of our road. In her brown mac, carrying a heavy black holdall, she reminds me of a refugee from the Second World War, trudging through the aftermath of the Blitz.

'Mum!' I call. She turns and waits for me, a faint scowl on her face. As I suspect, she was trying to sneak away unseen. 'The bus service isn't that bad,' I tell her. 'It won't take three hours to get to court. You've got time for breakfast, haven't you?' She glances back towards the house.

'I don't want to disturb Dani …'

'We don't have to. Wait in the car while I get dressed, and I'll take you to a café.'

I return to the house and put on the same clothes I wore last night. Mum is already waiting for me in the car, her seat belt buckled, her hands clasped demurely in her lap, her holdall on the back seat.

'I know I'm being a coward,' she says, her voice wavering slightly. 'But I know Dani will cry, and I'm not very good at dealing with tears. You'll explain that, won't you?'

'I will.'

We end up at a workman's caff on a nearby industrial estate. It never seems to close, which is why it is so popular with Chris and his colleagues after they finish a gruelling shift.

I order two belt-buster breakfasts, but neither of us do much more than push the greasy eggs and pork products around our plates.

We sit in silence for a few minutes.

'You won't do anything ... stupid while you're inside?' I ask. She shakes her head.

'I've got my meds packed, I'll speak to the prison doctor as soon as I can. I know my triggers, know what to look out for. I'm not going to let depression get a hold of me again.' She smiles defiantly and I recognise it as my own smile; the same smile I'd see staring out of the mirror as I hid in the staff toilets on my teaching placements, trying to psyche myself up sufficiently to face a tough crowd.

'Good,' I tell her, forcing myself to eat a piece of toast in order to feign nonchalance. 'We don't want you going anywhere.'

'I'm not going anywhere. I lost you once already. You were good to give me a second chance ...' Suddenly, unexpectedly, grief ambushes us both. We're sitting opposite one another with tears pouring down our cheeks. The workmen in the booth opposite look away, embarrassed, as we grab fistfuls of coarse paper napkins to mop up our tears.

'Oh God, what a mess we both are!' Mum is sobbing, but she battles through and forces her words out. 'The ... worst ... thing ... I ever did ... was letting them take you.' Some deep yogic breathing, and she's calm and centred once again. She leans over the table and takes my hands in hers. 'They took you away, and I was afraid that they'd take Dani too. I hid, because I was scared that they'd take both my babies away, that they'd start asking questions ... and they'd give you to your real dad. I know now that wouldn't have been possible, but when you're depressed you're not thinking rationally ...'

'I understand. But my real dad ...'

'Don't ask me about him, please.' She's still holding my hands, and the tears I cannot wipe away have dribbled down to my chin. Reaching up, her right thumb brushes them away deftly, then she takes my hands in hers once again. I try not

193

to notice the angry scars on her bare wrists. 'I've been a bad mum, and I know that this doesn't really undo all that I put you through. But I'm glad that I'm able to do it, and I feel better knowing that Dani's in good hands. You'll be such a good mum, Caitlin. You're nothing like me at all.'

'Well, if and when that happens, you'll definitely be out of prison. I'm not thinking about kids at the moment.'

'Well, if it happens, maybe I'll be a better grandma than I was a mum.'

Our food is so cold as to be past being edible. I go to the counter to pay, and we both go to the toilets to wash away any signs that we've been crying.

As we get back into the car, Mum says, 'If and when … You're changing your tune.'

'Well, I need a backup plan in case Geoffrey wheedles his way back into school.' I'm being flippant, but Mum takes me seriously.

'For what it's worth, you're amazing with Danielle. You and Chris should really consider having a family together.' No, we shouldn't. I don't want to even think about bringing children into a relationship that isn't built on honesty and trust. I've done a lot of bad things, a lot of stupid shit – but one of my redeeming qualities was that I was honest about my mistakes.

'Let me tell the truth,' I say to Mum, for the twentieth time. She shakes her head stubbornly.

'It's too late, Caitlin. I'm sorry you're still feeling guilty, but we agreed. This is what Dani wants. You have to look after her, and you have to let me do this …'

'But …'

'There's no point saying anything. It's your word against mine, and I've already pleaded guilty. You are *not* getting a criminal record, you are *not* losing your job and you are *not* going to prison. That's the end of it.' I can tell from her tone that this matter is no longer up for discussion. Where was this authoritative, bad-ass Mum when I needed boundaries and discipline? 'Anyway,' she adds coolly, 'you only did what I would have done if I'd been driving. Except I wouldn't have braked.' I'm rendered speechless. I literally don't know how to respond to that.

We drive straight to the County Court, even though there is over an hour before her sentencing begins. The building shares a car park with a local arts centre, and is already full to bursting.

'Why don't I drop you off outside, and then I'll go and find somewhere right at the back of the overflow car park?' I suggest. 'Save us dragging that huge holdall back across the car park.' I stop on some chevrons and hit the hazard lights.

'Good idea. Thanks, sweetheart. I'll see you soon.' Mum leans over and kisses me lightly on the cheek. She gets out of the car, and I see her in the rear view mirror, watching me as I drive away.

After driving round for five minutes I manage to find a parking space in the furthest corner of the car park; but almost as soon as I pull up the handbrake, a text message pings on my phone: DN'T COME TO COURT. ILL BE FINE. GO & CHECK ON DANIELLE AND YOULL HEAR FROM ME SOON. I LOVE YOU BOTH VRY VRY MUCH. XXX

She doesn't want either of us to see her in the dock. I have to respect that, because when I was facing my own sentence I couldn't bear the idea of Chris or Dani visiting me in prison.

I swallow the lump in my throat and reverse out, cursing the impatient motorist who is sitting, arms folded, waiting for me to vacate the parking space.

Chris sits in his car outside the house, waiting for me.

'Day off,' he says, presenting me with a bunch of carnations.

'Thought you might need the moral support, or at least someone to drive you to court.'

'She's already gone,' I tell him. 'She didn't want to hang around to say goodbye. I'm worried that Dani will take it hard.'

'She did. I gave her a lift to school, but she was in floods of tears. With hindsight, she should probably have stayed at home.' He puts his arms around me and rests his chin on the top of my head, enveloping me in his warmth. 'Are you okay?'

'I think so. I don't know.' I lean my head against his shoulder and bite down hard on my lip.

Just then, Dani bursts into the kitchen, clutching her mobile phone in her hand. She should have stayed at home after all.

'Mrs Graham tried to take it off me,' she says, waving the phone angrily. 'So I walked out of class. I've had this on refresh all morning.' She holds the device out to me, and I see the Law Pages website listing the morning's court cases and their verdicts. The first one reads: *ELSA BENNETT. Guilty plea. Sentenced to four years.*

'Perhaps she'll serve some of it on licence,' offers Chris. Danielle glares at him. I have a sneaking suspicion that Chris favoured a custodial sentence and thinks that four years isn't unduly harsh. A surprisingly large part of his job is cutting people out of cars after an RTC, and I know that he's seen a number of fatalities caused by drink or drug drivers, or even stupid dickheads texting while doing seventy on a dual carriageway.

I try to put my arms around Danielle, try to think of a way to comfort her, but she brushes me off, goes upstairs and slams the bedroom door behind her.

Chris embraces me again. I close my eyes and try to fight the tears welling in my eyes, but I'm not crying about the length of Mum's sentence. I'm crying because I feel so unworthy of his unswerving love and support. The slightest trace of a nightmare and he's awake, ready to hold me and cuddle me back to sleep. He phoned me once when I was fighting off a panic attack, and although I downplayed how sick and tense I was feeling, he sensed that something was amiss and turned up on the doorstep to check that I was okay. He's sat with me for hours in doctors' and solicitors' waiting rooms, dealt with Dani's emotional outbursts calmly, and never breathed a word that caused Mum agitation or upset, even though privately I know that he judges her for drink-driving. I couldn't have asked for anyone kinder, more understanding and supportive. These past few months would have destroyed some couples, but for me they have confirmed that Chris is the man I'm meant to spend the rest of my life with. Except that I'm no longer sure I can marry him.

Having the court case hanging over us meant that all engagement celebrations and wedding plans have been put on hold; but now it's over it's inevitable that discussions will turn towards our impending marriage. How can I marry him, promising to be true and loyal, when I'm lying to him?

I put these thoughts to the back of my mind and try to think of what Dani must be going through right at this moment. I go upstairs and knock softly on the bedroom door.

'What?' Dani asks, grouchily. I put my head around the door.

'Do you want to talk?' I ask. Her eyes are red from crying. 'Would it help you to hear a message from her?' Her brows pucker in a sarcastic scowl.

'Oh, she sent a message through you, did she? Wouldn't even hang around to say bye to me, but you got to go to court with her. Easy to see who's her favourite child!'

'That's not the case at all.' I push the door wide open and stand there, hands on hips. 'The opposite, in fact. She didn't say goodbye to you because it was too painful. It would have broken her heart. It's harder for her to leave you, because you're still her little girl and I'm a grown woman. But if it makes you feel better, she did a runner on me too – left me to park the car and then texted me to say I wasn't to come into court. You know it's not about favourites – it's just that she doesn't cope well with emotional situations.' I sit on the edge of the bed and pull Dani against me. Initially she resists, but then she leans her head against my shoulder and weeps. I stroke her soft hair and let her cry it out. 'We can go and see her soon,' I say, and this seems to calm her further. 'And Chris is right, she won't be behind bars for the full four years. She might be out before you start university.' But at the moment, with Danielle only going into Year 11, university seems light-years away.

A soft knock on the door. We look up and see Chris standing there, looking slightly bashful.

'I phoned the school and said Dani's not well and she won't be coming back in today. Hope I've not overstepped the mark or anything, but I didn't want the truancy officer ringing ...'

'It's fine,' I say, glancing at the clock. He's right – Mrs Court is cracking down on all unauthorised absences, and storming out of school could have brought about a visit from Dani's social worker. Chris smiles, but jerks his head towards the stairs.

'I'll be off, then. Give you two some space.' Dani slides off the bed and goes into the bathroom, leaving Chris standing in the doorway, looking at me. I see the concern in his dark, gentle eyes and there's a tightness in my chest. When he proposed he spoke of honesty and trust. No doubt he was thinking of his ex-wife's betrayal. I would never, ever hurt him like that; but it has occurred to me time and time again that concealing the truth from him is actually just another form of betrayal. If you love someone you are open with them and you share all your life with them. Sure, there are some things you might keep private – like when you got caught stalking your drop-dead-sexy history teacher, or that you once foolishly spent £200 on a pair of heels you couldn't walk in, or that you've been barred from a pub for throwing up over the barmaid ... But there's a line. If you've got a criminal conviction, huge gambling debts, a secret family, a serious addiction or blood on your hands – then that's a game-changer. You can't keep quiet about something which fundamentally affects your entire life. Because the debt, addiction, prison sentence, and all the lies you told in order to try and bury your problematic past – all those things can, and probably will, rise to the surface. That's if the guilt doesn't get you first.

'You're not okay, are you?' Chris asks. I shake my head and turn away from him, tears welling in my eyes. 'Cat, I hate seeing you like this. You've not been yourself since the accident. I'm worried you might have PTSD. Please, tell me what I can do to help.'

'You can't do anything,' I say, tearfully. 'It's all my fault.'

'No. You are not to blame for what happened, and neither is your mum. He came at you with a knife, for Christ's sake, he was trying to get into the car and drag you out. She was trying to stop you from being murdered ...'

'I did it,' I say quietly.

'Did what?'

'I was the driver.'

'You?' I nod my head. 'You ran him over?' There's no inflection in his voice, no change in body language for me to interpret.

'CAT!' Dani bursts out of the bathroom, screeching like a scalded cat. 'Why did you just tell him that? Why would you do that?' I turn and look at Chris.

'I can't lie to you any longer. I can't sleep, can't think straight, I'm having flashbacks ... and having to lie and cover things up is making it so much worse ...'

Dani cuts across me, 'So, you're choosing him over me? You said you'd never leave me, you promised I'd never be alone …' She jabs a finger at Chris, 'But now he'll go to the police and they'll send you to jail like Mum and … and…' She's almost hyperventilating. 'Shit, what if they send me to a young offenders' place, because I lied too? Oh my God, Cat, what have we done?'

'Dani …' Chris' voice is low and firm. She falls silent and looks at him, her cheeks white as a sheet. He holds up a finger, a sign for her to pause and take a deep breath. 'No one's going to prison. Could I speak to your sister alone for a minute?'

In the doorway she stops and fixes him with a tearful stare, a mute appeal for clemency.

'It's okay,' I tell her, gently. 'Whatever happens, Mum and I will take the blame. You had nothing to do with this.' She goes unwillingly, leaving the door open a crack. Chris goes to the door and closes it softly behind her so that she won't be able to eavesdrop.

'You were the driver?' he asks, still looking down at the door handle. 'Was it deliberate? Were you trying to kill him?'

'No. On my life, no. I did a three-point turn and tried to drive out of the cul-de-sac and he just stepped out in front of me … It happened exactly like we said in our police statements, except that I was driving, not Mum …' His shoulders slump, his posture sags. I cautiously interpret this release of tension as a good sign.

'And your mum took the blame to protect you?'

'I didn't want her to. We've fought over it, but she insists – I have to take care of Dani. This is her big shot at redemption for her, and a chance for me to stay on the straight and narrow. I don't see it that way, but as you saw, I'm outnumbered.' I sit on the edge of the bed and stare down at the carpet, giving him a chance to process everything. I slide my hands under my thighs and sit on them, to stop them from shaking.

'I think she's right,' he says, finally. I look up at him in shock. He sits on the edge of the bed, facing me.

'You do?'

'Yeah. If my girls had been through all the shit you've been through, then yeah, I'd go to prison for them, I'd lie for them, take the blame …'

'You would? Really?'

'If this happened to Alayah and Amy Rae, absolutely, I'd go to jail for them. And if it had happened to Dani instead of you, I suspect you'd do the same for her … Speaking of Dani, hadn't you better go and tell her that everything's okay?'

'We're okay? You're okay with what I've just told you?'

'If you'd just confessed to mowing him down in cold blood, then I'd be dialling 101 – but if you had meant to kill him, you wouldn't have said anything to me. Like you said, it was an accident. You didn't mean to hurt anyone, and neither did your mum. Neither of you deserve punishment – but I think after all she put you through, it's right that she protects you this once. Just don't ask me to take out life insurance before we get married, and we'll be fine.'

I continue to stare at him, unable to take in the fact that the cause of so many wakeful nights and panic attacks has just dissipated like chalk dust. He smiles, nervously. 'The life insurance was a joke. Not funny, I know, but you could at least humour my ego by pretending to smile.' I do smile. Relief floods through me like a warm cup of tea, and the fear in the pit of my stomach finally begins to thaw.

Dani opens the door and peeps through. Obviously, she has been listening to our entire conversation.

'So, we're okay, yeah?' she asks.

'I think we are,' says Chris, looking to me. I nod.

'We're okay,' I reply.

'Are you staying together? Still getting married?' I look at Chris, and it's his turn to nod. Dani claps her hands with gleeful relief. 'Do I still get to be your bridesmaid?'

'Do I have a choice?'

23

I can think of a hundred other ways I'd rather spend the weekend before my wedding, but I can't ignore the manager of the care home's urgent request for a meeting.

I'm on the A483 when Chris rings, furious after hearing from his ex-wife. She can't resist tugging on his strings occasionally, especially now she knows he's getting remarried.

'Cat, we've got a problem. Melissa just text me to say that the girls aren't allowed to come with us.' I sigh impatiently. I knew she'd try to throw a spanner in the works at the last minute, as she always does.

'Have you rung her?'

'Trying to calm down a bit first, so I don't say something I'll regret. I knew she'd try something like this, but to leave it to the day before we fly out, when I'm on my way to collect them … bloody hell!'

'Where are you now?'

'At the Birmingham services.'

'Keep driving south. Leave her to me.' I tap the button on my steering wheel and end the call, then use the voice-activated phone book to dial his ex-wife on my hands-free. I don't mind doing Chris' dirty work for him; in fact, aside from the odd teenage hissy-fit from Dani or a petulant pupil, these occasional verbal sparring bouts are now the only real source of conflict in my life.

'What do you want?' Melissa asks sourly. 'Chris sent you to fight his battles again?' She's another Geoffrey. I've never been anything other than courteous to her, and Chris, for his daughters' sake, displays the patience of a saint. I've lately come to the conclusion that not everybody is damaged or messed up. Some people are just inexplicably vile human beings.

'I understand you've just told Chris that he can't come and collect the girls.'

'Alayah has a swimming gala on Sunday. I'd forgotten about it until her coach reminded us that she had to attend.' She sounds so bloody smug and self-righteous.

'Well, that's going to cause a bit of a problem for us, because Chris is on his way down to collect the girls. The way I see it, Melissa, we can resolve this one of two ways: you can phone the coach, apologise profusely and explain that important though Alayah's swimming is, her father's wedding and a family holiday must take priority.' I'm grinning broadly to myself. Melissa hates when I use the word family. She can't deal with the fact that I'm not the evil stepmother, and that Alayah and Amy Rae actually enjoy spending time back in Wales. I adore them, mainly because their girlish enthusiasm for saccharine, soulless pop music has finally pushed Dani over to the dark side. She tries to scare them by playing emo music and wearing black lipstick; but to give her credit, she tolerates them uncomplainingly.

'Second option is this, Melissa: Alayah can go to her swimming gala, you can phone Chris and tell him that his six-hour round trip is a waste of time; the girls will miss being bridesmaids for their dad, they won't get to go on holiday, and we'll send you an invoice for the thousand pounds we've shelled out for dresses, passports, accommodation and flights. And believe me, I've paid for all those costs fifty-fifty, and I will recover my money.'

I'm met with a stony silence. It goes on so long that I'm tempted to ask whether she's still with me, but then she snaps, 'Fine, phone him and tell him they'll be ready for collection in an hour.'

'I will. And a word of advice before I go: Chris is a good dad. They love seeing him. If you stop them from having contact with him now, you might feel as though you're winning the

203

battle. But they'll remember, and they'll come to resent you for screwing them around. Don't ruin your own relationship with them for the sake of a few cheap shots at Chris.'

She hangs up. Preachy, yes, but she's had it coming for quite a while. I ring Chris back and tell him triumphantly that his girls will be coming with us, after all. Just as he's thanking me, I arrive at the residential care home, a large former manor house on the outskirts of Wrexham.

Let's get this over with quickly. I ring the doorbell and am greeted by the manager herself. She smiles, thinly, and shows me into her office. When I first visited to make arrangements I would be offered coffee, tea, hot chocolate and tissues, as 'it's often a very emotional time'. With each visit she has become noticeably less friendly.

The 'urgent issue' turns out to be nothing more than a repetition of what Dad's consultant told me when I last met with him a few weeks ago. The crash caused Dad's brain damage, but years of abusing his body with alcohol means that his internal organs have irreversibly deteriorated. Even if he were able to have a liver transplant, his advanced heart failure means that his lifespan is now being measured in months rather than years. I must sound appallingly cold-hearted as I reach into my briefcase, produce a copy of his most recent medical report and hand it to her, saying, 'Yes, his consultant explained all this to me at our last appointment. We've given permission for him to be transferred to hospital for any necessary medical care, and have a DNR in place. As a family we are as prepared as possible for his death.'

'We were thinking, perhaps you might like to make arrangements ... you know, for family and friends to say their goodbyes. He never has any visitors.' Not even his old drinking buddies have been to see him. I come to the care home to speak to the manager, but I have never visited Dad. The staff are aware of how he came by his brain damage, and probably think that I'm siding with the wrong parent. It was all over the news for a few weeks, sometimes disgustingly distorted: BLACK WIDOW MOWED HUSBAND DOWN WITH CAR. They've made a victim out of Dad and an aggressor out of Mum. How incredibly wrong they are – but that's what everybody seems to believe.

When the story made the news I was actually glad that Mum was behind bars – the only place where social media couldn't touch her. The names she was called on comments pages made my blood boil. It could have triggered a relapse for her.

'You didn't know my father before the accident,' I tell the manager. 'That's probably a good thing. He would have hated you. His alcoholism had alienated his entire family. At the risk of sounding like a heartless bitch, he's only reaping what he sowed over many years. If nobody visits and comforts him, that's entirely his own fault. I'm willing to make the funeral arrangements, but that is the only duty I feel bound to carry out for him.'

'I see,' she says, quietly.

'I don't think you do.' She looks up at me, and her expression has changed slightly, although I struggle to pinpoint the change.

'Will you see him, for a moment? Sometimes they hang on, you see, until they've had a chance to say goodbye. I know he can't express himself verbally, but he might want to make amends. It might bring you both some comfort ...'

I strongly doubt a meeting will be beneficial to either of us, but I mutely follow her up the stairs and onto the second floor. His room is right at the end of the building, with a beautiful double aspect of the gardens. It's a cheerful, pleasant room, in spite of the medical equipment and hoists which take up most of the space.

Dad is sitting in his chair, staring out of the window. A carer is writing something on his chart.

'Look who it is!' he says brightly, in his broken English. 'Your daughter, Mr Bennett!' The manager remains in the doorway and gives me an encouraging little smile. I approach the chair and stand at Dad's side. His eyes swivel towards me.

'Hi Dad, it's Caitlin,' I say, resting one hand on the back of the chair because I can't bring myself to touch his shoulder. 'I'm glad to see you so well looked-after.' He stares at me blankly for a second, unseeing, like a dog with cataracts. I wonder how much of him is still 'there' and how much is just functioning tissue. How much does he understand, how much can he remember? Is he still capable of rational thought? Does he seethe with silent indignation because I am the one who gave him this inescapable life sentence and evaded punishment? Or am I just a vaguely familiar face appearing through the fog, talking nonsense at him?

I speak to him as though I'm talking to a small child: 'I'm sorry to hear you've not been well. But I can see you're being taken very good care of, and I hope you're comfortable.'

Then, like the sun breaking through fog, I see it: he's still in there. It's perceptible only in a slight tightening of his jaw and a flicker of his eye, but somehow, his agitation is as loud as a shout. I see it in his eyes. He hates me, hates the fact that I'm the one calling the shots and looking after Dani while Mum is in prison; hates that I'm the one who put him in this chair; hates that I can get up and walk out of here while he's trapped for the rest of his time in a barely-functioning, immobile body. He can't communicate, can't control his bodily functions. Staring into those eyes, I get a glimpse of the hell he must be living.

One night, as Mum and I were sipping her disgusting Moroccan tea, she calmly told me, 'What's happened to him now is payback for all he did to us over the years.' Never again will he be able to hit another human being, raise a can to his mouth, or shout abuse. He spent so long trying to keep us in a state of helpless misery, and now he will never be able to hurt or bully another human being again.

Perhaps I imagined it, but Mum's lips may have curled into a slight sneer at the thought of the ironic 'justice' dealt to Dad. I think I might have been justified in agreeing that karma had given him a big kick up the backside for all the broken ribs, the slaps and punches, for all the days and nights I spent locked in the garage or the garden shed; however I don't share Mum's belief in karma. Life doesn't work like that. Life isn't fair.

'Goodbye, Dad,' I whisper. 'I hope you find peace.' I surprise myself by not only touching his shoulder, but by bending down and kissing his forehead. He jerks his head to the side, trying to escape the touch of my lips. His hatred towards me is entirely understandable.

I turn and leave without a backward glance, determined that this will be the last time I see him. I've asked Dani to come and sit with him, even for just a few minutes. She was the one thing in his life that he was able to take pride in, and possibly the only person he loved. But she won't come back here. The last time I suggested a visit she made her feelings very clear: 'He can rot in hell, and I hope he gets there soon!' I imagine he is already in his version of hell – sober, mute, clinical hell. He may already be dead to Dani, but as his legal next of kin I can't walk away so easily. Again with the irony: his bastard daughter, no blood relation, the person he hates most in the world is the one charged with managing his palliative care. If Dani won't visit him then inevitably he will die alone, or with a paid support worker at his side, because after today I am quite certain that my presence is an agitation. There will be no deathbed reconciliation, no forgiveness on either side. Let him die as he lived – blaming me for everything.

As I head towards the entrance the manager calls my name. She walks over, smiling a genuine, warmer smile.

'I'm sure that wasn't easy, but I think meant a lot to him. If there's anyone else you think might like to visit, please do encourage them to come along.' She lowers her voice to a whisper. 'And please ask them to come sooner, rather than later.'

I thank her again for the good care he's receiving, and then go back out to my car. I get in, belt up, and drive home. No tears or recriminations, no sitting slumped over the steering wheel, no introspective soul-searching.

I dreaded this meeting, but now it is over and done, I am surprised at how little I actually feel. A sort of numbness is entering my soul, wrapping itself around me like a protective chrysalis. During the past few months I've noticed that I feel less deeply and less strongly than I used to. Chris laughs and says I'm losing my youthful idealism and Dani says the anger management is finally working, but I know it comes from another place.

A few months ago the nightmares about being buried alive stopped and I began sleeping through the night again. Driving home, I realise that in spite of what Dad did to me, and in spite of what I did to him, I no longer feel anything resembling guilt, remorse or anger. I'm not sure whether this is healing or indifference, or whether there is actually any difference between the two.

Let Dad loathe me until he draws his last breath, I no longer care. The drunken sadist who beat me and broke my bones, tortured and loathed me – he is nothing to me now. The pain he inflicted and the rage he used to stir up inside of me – they have melted away. He has lost all his power over me, and I am free.

24

A few doors away from mine I hear muffled laughter. Chris and his brother are getting suited and booted, and probably enjoying a tipple as they dress.

Dani has worked her magic with her make-up pallet and styling appliances, and now I stand in front of the full length mirror as Chris' mother buttons up the back of my wedding dress. The row of pearl buttons finishes at the nape of my neck, and as she closes the last one I feel something light touching my skin. She is fastening a silver chain around my neck, deftly twisting it so that the diamond pendant falls to the front and lies in the hollow of my throat. Her eyes meet mine in the mirror's reflection.

'It belonged to my mother,' she whispers. 'Chris' grandma. She'd want you to have it.' I reach up and touch the stone with my fingertips to watch it catch the light. 'It's real,' she tells me. 'Only half a carat, but it's become a bit of an heirloom.' It could have come out of a Christmas cracker, for all I care. For me the value isn't in carats or clarity, but in the fact that she is choosing to entrust it to me. I turn and smile at her, struggling to repress my tears. Only the thought of Dani's wrath at my smudged mascara keeps me dry-eyed.

'It's absolutely beautiful. Thank you so much.' She touches my shoulder lightly, her smile sympathetic. I know she's feeling sorry for me, thinking that this is a difficult day to be without a mother. She's far too polite to ask any questions about my family, too afraid of being thought prying or nosy. But Chris said that his explanation as to why we wanted a quiet, family-only wedding reduced her to tears.

'Is there anything else I can do for you, sweetie?'

'No, thank you. Dani will be here in a moment and we're just about ready.'

'If there's nothing left for me to do, I'll see you downstairs.' She leaves, struggling to cross the polished wooden floor in her high heels.

I go to the vanity case on my dressing table, take out the little square of white card and read it to myself, although by now I know the words by heart. My vows, and all the reasons I want to spend the rest of my life with Chris. I go to slip it into my little handbag, along with tissues and lipstick; and in doing so I notice that I have a new text message on my phone.

The message is from Mrs Court. I was going to invite her to join the wedding party, but when I mentioned that it was going to be a small, intimate ceremony abroad she replied, 'That will be perfect for you. Just Chris, his family, you and Danielle. You don't need the fuss of a big entourage, and you've never belonged to anybody so you certainly don't need anybody to give you away.' There was something about the way she delivered that comment, a slight edge to her tone. Perhaps she was telling me that she wasn't expecting an invite or that she would have found it awkward to be mentor and mentee on holiday together. Perhaps she was worried that I would ask her to be a stand-in parent out of some mawkish sense of obligation, or even that her presence would spoil things for Danielle. Perhaps, having lost her own husband prematurely, she was worried about how she would react to all the romance and happily-ever-after. Whatever the reason, she made it gently apparent that the invite needn't be issued. Reading her text message, I feel a pang of regret that I didn't invite her anyway.

> *Thinking of you both today, at the start of a wonderful and exciting adventure. God bless you both. (Also WONDERFUL news re. school. Details to follow.)*

I place my phone back on the dressing table and find myself staring out of the window, down into the walled garden where Alayah and Amy Rae are being chaperoned by their grandfather. They are walking in stately circles and earnestly scattering imaginary flowers in rehearsal for the ceremony.

'I should have got a flower basket too.' I turn to see Dani standing in the doorway, a mock scowl on her face. 'Think they're so bloody cute ...'

'They are,' I tell her. 'They're adorable. But you're beautiful.'

'Don't you go getting all mushy on me,' she mutters, going to the chest of drawers and taking out the flat box containing my veil. As she stands there smoothing the creases out of the tulle I find myself watching her, my throat taut and my eyes stinging with the effort of repressing tears of pride at what a beautiful, elegant yet feisty young woman my little sister is maturing into.

Holding the veil by the comb, she approaches me and slides the pearl base into my scalp. She arranges the layers so that they hang in folds around my head, and as she draws the veil down to cover my face, our eyes meet.

'Will you walk me up the aisle?' I ask her.

'Like, give you away?' I nod, my throat still taut. She answers my nod with one of her own, and a shy smile. Then her mouth quivers and suddenly we're both in tears. She throws her arms around me and we hold one another tightly. It's a strange moment, this feeling of being caught between joy and grief – relief at having survived the worst years of our youth, and sorrow that we've both paid such a heavy price to reach this point. We cling to one another as tightly as drowning sailors cling to driftwood. She has been the one constant in my life, my source of strength, my blood and my best friend.

There's a knock on the door followed by a cry of, 'Five minutes, ladies!'

'Coming!' I call, as we separate and reach for the tissues to dab at our damp eyes. Dani gathers up her posy and my bouquet, and I reach for my white satin handbag.

'How's my make-up?' I ask, glancing worriedly at my eyes.

'Good to go. I used waterproof mascara.' Slowly she turns 360 degrees and asks, 'How does my dress look?'

'Perfect. Mine?'

'Even more perfect. Are you ready?' I take a deep breath and turn to glance one last time at my reflection in the mirror.

Then my phone begins to vibrate on the wood of the dressing table. I pick it up, surprised at having any incoming calls because it's a new number and I haven't given it out to many people. The caller profile is greyed out and the word WITHHELD flashes beneath it.

'Sales call. Ignore it,' says Dani. I stare down at the screen, feeling instinctively that something isn't quite right. All scam and marketing calls appear as numbers, because I always make a point of googling and blocking them. The only phone calls I get from withheld numbers are … Dani appears to share my train of thought, because she looks up at me and we say almost simultaneously:

'Prison.'

'The care home.'

I look down again at the phone in my hand. The call has ended, but within a few seconds the caller rings again. Somehow, I just know that the call won't bring good news.

'Don't answer it,' Dani says. My thumb twitches, but I don't swipe right. 'Not now. Not while we're happy.'

Whatever has happened, whatever may be happening, is beyond our control. We're in France – too far away to be of any practical use or to make a dash to hospital. But more than that, Dani is right – there will always be problems. Right now, in this moment, we are happy. Whatever sorrow awaits us can wait just a little longer. Right now I am with the girl I love most in the world, and I am about to marry the man I love most in the world. Nothing is going to change that. Nothing is going to spoil today.

The phone stops vibrating and the voicemail icon flashes up on the screen. I place it back on the dressing table and reach instead for my bouquet of pink and lilac roses. Once more, Dani drapes the veil so that it lies lightly across my face, and goes to smooth the train of my dress.

'Ready?' she asks. I slide my arms through hers and clasp the bouquet to my waist. Arm in arm with my sister, I depart without a backwards glance.

~